Where the Time Goes

Hardscrabble Books — Fiction of New England

Other Books by R. D. Skillings

In a Murderous Time
P-town Stories
Alternative Lives

R. D. Skillings

Where the

TIME GOES

University Press of New England

HANOVER AND LONDON

University Press of New England publishes books under its own imprint and is the publisher for Brandeis University Press, Dartmouth College, Middlebury College Press, University of New Hampshire, Tufts University, and Wesleyan University Press.

University Press of New England, Hanover, NH 03755
Printed in the Unites States of America

5 4 3 2 1

Library of Congress Cataloging-in-Publication Data
Skillings, R. D. (Roger D.), 1937–
  Where the time goes   /   R.D. Skillings.
    p.   cm. — (Hardscrabble books)
  isbn 0–87451–939–x (pbk. :   alk.paper)
  1. New England—Social life and customs—Fiction. I. Title. II. Series.
ps3569.k48w48   1999
813'.54—dc21   99–19856

Acknowledgments: "The Line" first appeared in *Shankpainter*; "The Present" in *The Northwest Review*; "Silence" and "Czezarley Zoo Gets Out" in *The Harvard Review*; "No Escape for Yours Truly" in *Zone 3*; and "Ghosts," as a poem entitled "Manny," in *The Silverfish Review*. I thank the editors of these journals.

To the old P-town. Gods bless the new.

Contents

Where the Time Goes

That's P-town

A guy came in Silk & Feathers the other day, he cruised around a while, then he took something off the rack and went in the dressing room to try it on.

When he came out he went right up to me and said, "How does this look?"

He had a skirt on sideways with his prick hanging out where the zipper was.

I said, "You're acting out. You can't come in here if you're going to act out. I'll have to call the police if you keep on acting out."

He said, "Acting out? What do you mean acting out?"

I said, "If you drip on that you just bought it."

I mean, this is a dress shop. What was a man doing in here anyway?

Breakfast Anyone?

I am sixty-five years old, I don't get laid much, but that's all right. This morning I was down on the beach dumping out some rotten soup for the gulls. I stood around, washing the pot, watching the sun come up.

When I came back on the deck, my downstairs neighbor—she's very cute, she's forty-eight, she's in AA, hasn't had a drink in seven years—she's got this muffin she just took out of the oven. It's still in its tinfoil wrapper. I can see the stream rising. She's got it in both hands, she's holding it out for my breakfast like it's in a chalice. She's got these sort of potholder gloves on, she's looking great, she's looking really, really happy.

I had to say, "You'd better tell me what's in it. I have all these allergies. I have to be careful."

So she lists all these perfectly nice ingredients, and wouldn't you know, one of them was walnuts.

I said, "Oh, God, I'm sorry, but if I ate that I'd probably die."

She almost cried, she didn't really cry, but something happened to her eyes. I saw it. They sort of squinched up and then she wiped them with the crook of her elbow, she was still holding this damn muffin in the air, perfectly beautiful muffin.

There wasn't much to say after that. This whole year we've hardly spoken a word. I come stumbling in at all hours of the day or night.

There were a million things I could have said, none of which occurred to me at the time. Now I'm in mourning.

The Line

Emily hadn't been back to Provincetown for almost two years, and once she escaped the stifling bus, forged her way up Commercial Street through the teeming, noonday scene and got sat down with her coffee and bag of dope in Virginia's crammed, even-hotter studio, she couldn't stop talking.

"Some busybody saw an article in the *Globe* about some shelling and called my mother—this person wasn't even really a friend, she just happened to remember the name of my kibbutz.

"My mother's a little old lady in Brighton with two locks on every door and you can't open the windows anymore because she's been mugged twice. It's the last decent apartment in the building. The rest are all broken up for college students, and the landlord's trying to drive her out.

"My mother finally got me on the phone 'No, Mother, I'm perfectly all right,' I said and hung up. It costs seven dollars a minute, she can't afford that."

Emily inspected the fat joint she had rolled. "I don't even know where the bomb shelters are. You just duck. Americans are so stupid, they don't even know there's war on. I feel guilty about having left, especially since everything's getting so much worse lately, but I made my reservations five weeks ago."

"Where do you get off with this guilt trip," Virginia said. "You're not a Christian."

"I know," Emily said. "Well, I wanted to see my mother. I'm only staying three weeks. That's about all I can stand."

"I know what you mean," Virginia said. She never looked up from the piece she was painting, which she turned in her lap. The studio and most of the rest of the apartment were crowded with brightly colored papier-mâché sculptures of herself, her friends and acquaintances, pet dogs and public figures; floor to ceiling the walls were covered with paintings of the same subjects. Richard Nixon with bulbous nose and nervous teeth hunched in his suit waving both hands with V-for-Victory signs. The caption read, *I am not a crook.*

"You probably think I'm crazy," Emily said. They had gone to art school together, come to P-town summers, and then never left and lived the life, the bars and men, drugs and drink. But Emily, who had a daughter, little by little had defected, had become a cook on a fishing boat, had traveled, while Virginia had stayed in her studio for ten years.

"Yeah," she said with quiet asperity. "It does sound kind of crazy."

They were sitting side by side near the door in the last semicircle of empty space. The entire apartment was almost full, and soon once again would intrude the need for a larger place. Already one had to duck *The Mad Bomber with a Crewcut* to get into the bathroom, and her poet-husband's book-crammed cell housed a beautiful six-foot atomic mushroom spread over dead cockroaches the size of newborn babies.

Emily lit the joint, tasted it, squinted, took a big hit, and passed it to Virginia, who shook her head. "I quit," she said.

"You quit?" Emily said. "I don't believe it. This is not possible."

"Well, I get desperate sometimes," Virginia admitted, her custom having been to smoke pot while she worked, which was all day long.

"And you haven't had a drink in five years either," Emily said, properly awed and respectful.

"Yeah," Virginia said, a little awed herself. "So what have you been doing?"

"Well, mostly just work. I don't have much time. It isn't easy. Let me see. Well, I was doing some drawings, sort of like Degas."

"That's what you were doing when you left," Virginia said in exasperation. "What you're saying is nothing's changed."

"Well, I don't know," Emily said dubiously. She had grown lean as a man and had an older, weathered look, with new lines in her face and grey hairs. She had never looked better. Virginia herself looked rosier and younger than ever. The sweat ran down her nose. She put aside the piece she was working on and picked up another. Outside the window white blossoms and fuzzy, spade-shaped leaves muted the light and the passing voices. Downstairs on her door was her constant sign: *Do Not Disturb.*

Emily handed her the joint. She took a long toke, handed it back, and went on touching up a fish with a red head and a large silver eye.

"War's no good," Emily said, "especially for women and children."

"I can't understand what you're doing there," Virginia said.

"I don't know myself," Emily said, passing Virginia the joint again. "All I know is I'm going back a week from today."

Virginia put down her brush and had a good blast at the last of the roach, handed it back and then, horrified, cried, "What am I doing? I'm supposed to be quitting. I hate the stuff. I loathe and detest it."

"I never smoke over there, it makes me too paranoid," Emily said.

"What have you got to be paranoid about?" Virginia said. "I thought guilt was your trip."

"Fear of bombs. Artillery," Emily said with a certain complacence. "Death."

"The Big Bummer, eh?" Virginia said, absentmindedly having a puff of the new joint, squinting through the smoke. "Fear of insanity. You haven't met that one yet."

Emily laughed. "No, I don't worry much about that."

"How's your love life?" Virginia asked.

"I don't have one, thank god," Emily said. "There's no time for that."

"Where's all your exs?" Virginia said.

"Fishing, I guess," Emily said. "You probably know better than I do."

"Fred's the only one I ever see," Virginia said. "He went dry for quite a while but he got bored." She had two quick tokes before she remembered. "Stop! What am I doing? I hate this stuff. I've quit. Keep it away from me."

"Sorry," Emily said. "I keep forgetting."

"Yeah," Virginia said. "Fred was all right when he was sober."

"He liked to scheme," Emily said. "He'd rather do anything than work. He lived in fear of jail."

She passed the joint to Virginia who had a puff and passed it back but neither noticed. They hardly glanced at each other. Emily was engrossed in all the new paintings and sculptures. Virginia was replenishing her palette.

"How's McEll and Ida?" Emily asked.

"They're fine," Virginia said, "so long as only one of them's in town at a time. McEll's running the shop. Ida's up in Vermont. They can't stand to be together down here. It drives them crazy. They got married again."

"Again?" Emily said. "You're kidding."

"Yeah," Virginia said. "They had to. They got too jealous."

"Well, at least they haven't killed each other yet," Emily said. "How's Loretta?"

"Loretta!" Virginia said, and put down the head she was painting. "Loretta went berserk finally. She punched a cop. She's vicious. She made a pass at me. Can you imagine! I was sitting with her in the Fo'c'sle, she put her hand right in my lap, I had to leave. You don't even want to go near her. She kissed some guy, some poor tourist, and bit a big hole in his lip. There was blood all over the place."

"What's with her?" Emily said.

"I don't know," Virginia said. "She had this weird look in her eyes. She kept saying, 'I've finally gone over the line. Come on over, I know you will sooner or later. It's nice over here. Come on over. You'll love it.'"

"Jaysus!" Emily said.

"Everybody's gone over the line," Virginia said. "Have you seen people pushing these little alligators on wheels in the street? They stop and have fights with them. All the dykes have dyed their hair purple. You can't believe how decadent it is. I don't even go out anymore."

"Well, I'm going back to Israel," Emily said.

"Right now?" Virginia said.

"No, right now, I'm going to the Fo'c'sle," Emily said.

"And have a few shooters," Virginia said with raillery tinged with nostalgia.

"Just a few," Emily said definitely. She slipped a new joint into her pack of Camels and got up, taking a last look around the studio. "I'll come by tomorrow."

"Why?" Virginia said. "Why, why are you going back?"

"I don't know," Emily said. "I should be there now."

Coughlan Dice at His Closet Window

Donald's back, I'd guess, this time for good. Only a week and already he's walking the wall, back and forth, back and forth, morning, noon and night, as if he'd never been away. I've lost count of his settings out.

But he's always welcomed back, always gets his old job back at a cousin's fast-food stand. No dismay in people's eyes, I'm sure, no questions asked. He's back that's all, and they're glad to have their born faith confirmed that there's nothing up there beyond the bridge, nothing worth leaving town for.

They're not surprised to see him on his wall, though I'll bet no one takes note but me, that he's no whit less perfectly balanced than he was through all his placid years of school, arms outstretched, heel set at tip of toe precisely, almost fastidiously, clocklike, slow and sure.

He never fell the ten feet down to the parking lot my desk looks on. I learned not to worry, never saw him hesitate or sway, jig about, kneel or sit to outwait panic's vertigo. His shambling hulk's ungainly on the street, graceful on that wall.

I think he loves it up there, feels alone. I watched him grow from child to boy to man at six foot four, 220 pounds, and then he disappeared again, and then I heard he'd gone to M.I.T.

And now he's back, failed promise unlamented, back again among his phlegmatic townsmen, known like his father to have a flair for figures, small use of course, though doubtless he can still when in the mood to flabbergast perform fantastic mental feats, beat the pants off a pocket calculator, or recite every word of every page he read or heard last week or year.

But he wasn't happy there, I fancy, couldn't cope with grades or dormitory life or quick-tongued girls in Harvard Square. Here he's got a home, a mother and a sister nondescript as himself, a lame brother he helps along, and his father, a volunteer fireman, and mainstay of the rescue squad, imperturbable, plain-spoken patriarch with such powerful eyesight and knowledge of the bay where he once fished—back when there were fish—that he can pinpoint landmarks no one else can see, much less know where to scan the misty emptiness and dim shoreline. He's prouder of this native knack than of his unplumbed depths of math and memory his world takes for small abnormality, himself included.

The son too is reputed to have strong eyes, and stops and stands sometimes pensively gazing at what or where I cannot guess.

In all these years I've only had with him just one, brief, exchange of words about which assemblage of pizza toppings would best slake my raging appetite, add least to my great waddling girth, even then three hundred pounds—I'm only five foot ten—and bore away with my wind-buffeted box a daunting sense of calm, of a spirit unassuming, courteous, kindly, intelligent, private like his father, mild beings both, gone down their casual paths, doubles of a destiny unguessed, unprized, unmissed.

It always made me sad to ponder what they might have been, yet today—my desk a mass of faded pages scrawled with second thoughts, repudiated ends, new beginnings, murky consequences, all my fondest inklings snarled, outgrown, betrayed, old ambition's head long shamed from sight—what hard-won skill and bitter discipline would I not trade for grace like theirs at least to own my nature, love or not, adapt or shed my lethargy, act or settle for some fine, high solitude in this ill-starred enterprise, my life?

Well, another day's done, must be done. Here he comes, bird's arms outstretched to fly. But he won't. He doesn't think of flying, has no need or want of sky. Why should he? What could he eat of air, what else crave than dinner's sated sleep. Well, no more do I!

Yes! One of my own grand carbonaras, some crisp and spicy greens, a clean Tuscan white, a pint of raspberry sorbet, a pot of freshly ground strong coffee, and a long beguiling night on my couch in pajamas with cannabis, good TV, and no qualms about the future, please.

He does keep trying though. I wonder who he talks to. I suppose some day he'll get a wife. And children too. Why should I mourn? He's nothing like me, more my foil. And yet there's something else of him I can't help but marvel at—amid so much junk food he never snacks. He told me that.

I could hardly believe it. I'd be what? A mountainous buffoon. Everybody's friend.

Among the Condo Dwellers

I was trying to escape into TV. We were right in the middle of one of our typical condo brouhahas. They're driving me nuts. The Chairman of the Committee keeps calling me up—what color mailboxes are allowed, what kind of flowers should be in everybody's windowboxes, does everything everyone has have to be exactly the same?

Gary and Philip put a yellow lightbulb over their back door and that caused an uproar. They didn't do it to provoke. That was just the only color bulb they happened to have, and now they've dug in their heels to keep it. They think it's mad not to be able to do even the least little thing without Committee permission.

There's a big fad for uniformity, but nobody can agree on what it should be. So everything has to be hashed over and voted on, but there're only four units, since I rent and don't count, and my landlords are in Paris and refuse to get involved.

Everybody keeps calling me up to complain about the others and get my sympathy or win me over to their side, never mind that I can't vote. All the owners have strong opinions—about condo affairs, if nothing else—and they're always at an impasse. They're getting to hate each other and each thinks the others are out to thwart him. Every time a new question comes up they switch alliances. But it's always a tie, two against two. I can never tell who's not speaking to whom, it's making me dizzy.

I never watch daytime TV. I was just trying to block out all these hysterical phone calls. They're making me a hypocrite. I have to commiserate, I have to pretend to agree with all sides. I know I'm going to end up with all enemies.

Anyway, a newsflash came on. This terrible plane crash in Milwaukee. It happened right near the airport. You could see the smoke. There were all these eyewitnesses. Like spectators. And swarms of newspeople with camcorders interviewing them. I wanted to turn it off but I couldn't. I think I was afraid the phone would ring.

One man saw the whole thing. He said the plane went straight down. He could see passengers beating their fists on the windows.

Then they flicked to a special room in the airline terminal where all the people who'd come to meet the flight were gathering. An airline representative was trying to prepare them for the news. He looked very young for that job, very nervous. He kept folding and unfolding his hands in front of his belt. Finally he just let them hang there. People were still going in and taking seats. The press was milling outside, trying to get in.

One woman came running, pulling a little girl by the hand. She was trying to ward off the microphones with a magazine. It was like a receiving-line gauntlet. At the door she suddenly shied away and went to one of those enormous tinted windows. Way off over the horizon of tarmac you could see a little thin tentacle of smoke that smeared out on top like a black lily pad. The child was about eight years old. She looked just like my niece.

I grabbed the phone and called my sister. I knew they weren't on that flight. I knew they were home, where they always are on a Saturday noon. They were fine of course. She was fine. Jim was fine. Melody was fine. Ma was in her usual snit about the bee in Pop's bonnet about buying an island and moving us all to the Seychelles.

We talked a long time about nothing at all. I never told her why I called. But I've felt sick ever since. I can't bear it. That's the truth.

Job Ops

Would you like to hear how I fell off the wagon? Do you think you can stand it? I hadn't had a drink in a month. I was all cleaned up. I had a haircut, my hand didn't shake anymore, I could get a cigarette lit without giving myself away, I'd been eating like a horse, I'd been to the laundry, shaved off my beard, bought a new shirt, pressed a pair of pants.

I was swilling ginger ales in the Bradford one day. Bob was bartending. I says, "You wouldn't happen to know of any jobs, would you?" I told him all my requirements. No dishwashing. I gave him the whole resume. I didn't want to work too many hours. No mornings. I didn't want to have to stand up all day, I didn't want to have to work too hard. Reasonable pay, reasonable employer. Something nice and sane, suitable for myself. A little chumpchange to go with my social security. I need a year-round place. I don't want to spend another summer on the beach.

The very next day I was in there again. Bob says, "Oh, by the way, I heard of the perfect job for you." And he gave me a rundown. I couldn't believe the salary. It was the best job I ever heard of in this town. It was made in heaven for me. I thought to myself, This is my rightful reward. Getting off the booze at my stage of life is not child's play. The d.t.'s are not fun. Maybe there is such a thing as justice.

I says, "Where's this job?"

He says, "I don't know. I didn't ask."

I says, "Who told you?"

Bob says, "Guy who came in."

"Who?" I says. "What's his name?"

Bob lifts his cap off and scratches his head. He screws it back on and rubs his eyebrows. He looks out the window. I'm holding my breath. "It's slipped my mind," he says.

"You'll think of it," I says. "What's he look like?"

"Ordinary-looking guy," Bob says. "He almost never comes in anymore. Year or two since I've seen him."

"Did you tell him about me?" I says.

"Sorry," Bob says. "If I see him again I'll mention your name."

"You know my name?" I says.

"Yeah!" he says. "Of course. I'll think of his name, don't worry."

I sat there for two hours watching him make drinks. He couldn't think of the name. "Never mind," I says. "You're trying too hard. It'll come to you. Don't strain the brain. Let it work in its own time."

"Don't worry," he says.

I spent the whole afternoon there, more of a stretch than I would ever have done if I were drinking. My mouth was watering for that job. All my troubles would be over. Nice new life. A home. A shelf for my books now stashed in boxes all over town. Wall space for my prints rolled up for the last umpteen years. My own bed. All that.

He couldn't think of the name. He says, "I'm no good at names. They go in one ear, out the other."

"Listen," I says. "This is serious. You've got to think of this guy's name. Before he gives the job to someone else."

"Well," Bob says, "he wasn't the one with the job anyway. He just told me about it."

"So who had the job?" I says quick, trying to take him by surprise, jar it out of his memory.

"I don't know," Bob says. "I never knew that. He never told me."

"Well, think!" I says. "Try to remember the guy's name who came in."

"Yeah," he says. "All right. Okay. I'll try."

Of course, he's busy. I keep exhorting him, I'm practically begging him, and he's getting annoyed. "What more do you want me to do?" he says.

"Think," I says. "For god sakes, think!"

"I am," he says. "Quit worrying about it. Cool it for a little while."

So I went home and waited a few hours. I ransacked my mind for who it might be. I couldn't imagine anyone I knew personally having a job like that, or even knowing anyone who had a job like that, but I was determined to consider every face I could conjure up. Quite a crew!

I went back to the Bradford. Bob was just getting off, having his drink of the day. "Not yet," he says. "Sometimes I feel as if it's on the tip of my tongue, and then it sort of melts. I never had much use for memory anyway. Most things I'd just rather forget. Know what I mean?"

"All too well," I says. I was trying my best not to get him aggravated. I was afraid to pester him. I says, "Sleep on it. It'll be there in the morning."

"Yeah," he says. "You might be right. But I don't know."

His tone made my heart sink. "Listen," I says, "you can't give up."

"Yeah," he says. "I'll try." But I can see he's got other things on his mind. For instance Julie, who's just broken up with Gabe. Bob's had his eye on her for years.

I went home. I didn't sleep a wink. I was waiting at the Bradford when they opened. It turned out to be Bob's day off. I waited around, and of course about noon he showed up with Julie. They took their drinks to a table. They were very engrossed. I restrained myself as long as I could. When he got up to get another round I sidled over.

"Hey!" he says. "How're you doing?"

"Bob!" I says. "Don't you remember?"

"Oh, yeah," he says. "Yeah, yeah!"

I said, "Please!"

"All right, all right," he says. "I'll try. I'll keep trying."

So I went and sat at the bar till they left. On their way out I sort of casually intercepted them at the door. He just shook his head at me and shrugged.

I was back first thing in the morning. He's putting out the fruit, cutting up the limes. "Naw," he says. "I can't remember."

I almost couldn't believe it. I could see this damn job seeping away. I never wanted a job in my life like I wanted this job. "Look," I says, "let's see if we can figure out this guy's name. Did it begin with *A*? Allen? Arnold, Arthur?"

"No," he says. "Didn't begin with *A*."

"Bill," I says. "Buster. Bob. Maybe it's Bob. That's why you've blocked it."

"Wasn't Bob," he said. "I'd remember that. Wasn't *B* anyway."

"*C*," I says.

"No," he says. "Wasn't *C*. I don't think."

We went through the alphabet. He shakes his head on every letter. I says, "It's got to be one of them."

"I guess," he says. "Certainly wasn't *Z* though."

Four days this went on. I'm living in fear that it's getting too late. He says, "I guess I smoked too much dope in the old days."

We went over the guy's description about a thousand times. Dark hair. Not exactly black, not brown either. Somewhere in between. Clean shaven. Ordinary clothes. Whatever that means. "I see a lot of people," Bob says.

Apparently the guy didn't have a single distinguishing feature.

Eyes blue. Maybe brown. Medium size, medium height. One absolutely generic joe with the best job in the world. I was exhausted. Bob was bored silly even though I let up on him for hours at a time. I'd go across the street to the Old Colony and nurse a few ginger ales and then I'd come back and pretend I wasn't just waiting for him to remember the magic name.

One time I came back in, I was actually proud of my selfcontrol, of how long I'd been gone. He said to Kimball Tardiff out of the side of his mouth, "Ohhh, noo!"

Kimball had had a few. "Hey," he says, "I hear you've got a memory problem."

"It's no joke," I says.

"I'll say," Bob says.

"*You'll* say," I says.

"No offense," he says.

"Work," Kimball says, "is the curse of the drinking classes. Be thankful. No job would suit you. Take it from me."

Of course he just got done painting all morning. I don't know how he does it.

I think it was about the fifth day, it was absolutely quiet, early in the week, nobody around, just me and Bob there looking out the window. Every man that goes by I'm praying Bob's going to say, "That's him!"

After a while I realized I hadn't seen a soul I knew myself. Just anonymous faces. All of a sudden Bob snaps his fingers. He screws his hat down tight. He glares at me. I'm waiting and waiting. He says, "I just figured out why I couldn't remember the guy's name."

I look back at him. I'm about ready to croak.

"I never knew it in the first place," he says. "I knew my memory wasn't all that bad."

"Well, that's a relief," I says.

We look out the window for a while. It's a gorgeous day. A few snow flurries. Last of the spring. The wind's blowing them around every whichway. Up down round and round. All shot through with sun.

Finally he says, "Sorry I put you through all this. I really am. I wish there was something I could do for you. I really do. If you ever think of anything, anything at all, anything within my power to do, I'll do it, just let me know."

I said, "Give me a beer."

Czezarley Zoo Gets Out

Two workmen came down the steps of the Cellar Bar at a half trot, took stools by the door, got Budweisers, pushed their glasses away and began to drink without speaking, bottles rising and falling spasmodically, like pistons, almost in unison, and neither moved an eyelid when a distraught woman came in and sat down beside the shorter, stockier one.

"Dick!" she said. "Dickie!"

He swung on his stool, knees banging hers. "Why didn't you just go and get yourself fucked?" he said straight out.

"What?" she said. "Oh, Dickie, that's ridiculous!"

"Yeah?" he demanded, then faced front again. Lush black curls escaped a watch cap pulled tight over his skull. He was about thirty, but already his expression had settled into a vehement gloom, though sly, cynical, little hooks remained in the corners of his sometimes-still-boyish smile.

His lanky companion had never seemed young, had a lined forehead and harried air, kept sullen attention, glowering at the shelves of bottles before them.

"He's a friend of mine, you didn't have to walk off like that," the woman said. She might have been twenty-five and wore baggy jeans and a sweatshirt, was big breasted, nearly an inch taller than either man despite her slouch, and her eyes were wary, soft and glazed.

"You always stop to talk to niggers on the street?" Dick pursued. "You got friends like that, you don't need me."

"Oh, Dickie, don't be like that!" she pleaded, trying to laugh. "You're not from Alabama."

"If I was I'd be twice as worse."

"You see!" she cried. "You know it's wrong."

"I don't know nothing," he said. "I know I can't stand niggers."

"Oh, God!" she said. "You sound just like my father."

"Yeah? And what would he think of you now?"

"I don't know," she answered after a moment abstractedly, disconsolate in her whole being. When had that man ever had a clue, or her mother either, for all it mattered? She felt so sorry to be always alone.

"That's right!" Dick loudly apprised the whole bar. "She don't give a fuck for her own father."

"Oh, please," she appealed to the other man, "tell him to stop being ridiculous."

Dick's friend tensed, but didn't turn his head, spoke his mind ponderously, spacing his words: "The way I see it is this. I got nothing against Negroes so long as they keep to themselves."

"You're two of a kind," she said with an edge of resigned contempt.

"You're God damned right!" he said like driving nails.

"Why didn't you just go and get laid when you had the chance?" Dick followed on in a hard, quiet tone.

"You don't have to talk that way," she said.

"Where was you going before we came along?" Dick demanded.

"I was just out for a walk," she said, plaintive at a tolerable day gone crazily wrong.

"Yeah?" Dick said. "Why don't you just go now and finish what you started?"

"Oh, Dickie, you really, really, really don't have to say things like that."

"You don't know," Dick said. "You don't know nothing. I seen you looking at him."

"If you were from Alabama!" she said, furious tears welling.

"Get out of here!" Dick said, hollow amazement aching his chest. "Just get out!"

"Dickie," she said, "it's me, Doris."

"I said you were sweet," he said, shutting his eyes, "but not that sweet."

"Oh, Dickie, please, please, please don't be riciculous," she begged.

But his face was contorting, darkening, puckering like an exposed brain, and she stood up and backed away.

"I can't stand the sight of you," he said, his voice near cracking, his eyes squeezed to slits. He banged both elbows on the bar, whopped his ears with his fists. A bottle toppled and rolled but didn't fall off. The bartender stood up. The other patrons huddled away in corners.

She reeled past the two stolid backs and went through the open door, stumbling up the cement steps to the street.

The two men went on staring straight ahead. The bartender sat down and put on a mask of absence.

"I just can't hold it in," Dick said, "I know I should, but sometimes I just can't." He wiped his eyes with his sleeve.

"You did just right," said the other, half hugging, half shaking him with one arm. "I always keep quiet and end up hating myself. I respect you a whole lot, man, for what you just did."

"I'm not prejudiced," Dick said. "I don't think I'm prejudiced, but there's one thing I can't stand."

"White girls and niggers," the other said.

"The way it's going we'll all be brown."

"We got to stop it somewhere."

Dick shook his head and said, "Last time I was in Boston, I was in this cafeteria and these two niggers, they was nothing but kids, they yanked some old drunk out of his chair, he must've said something to them I guess, and they stomped him and everybody just sat there."

"Nobody did nothing?"

"No. They just walked to the door and one said, 'He's all right, don't worry about him'. And the second guy says, 'Is he, is he all right?' and ran back and stomped him in the face again. Then they just walked out. Nobody did anything. They just let the old guy lie there."

"I wish I'd been there," the man said, but he didn't sound sure.

Dick bowed his head, then snapped it up. "I feel bad about Doris. For a moment there I could've killed her. I think I really could've, I was scared."

"I know. It makes you feel bad, white girls and niggers. People got feelings. She should know that."

"I got feelings," Dick said with heart-broken defiance.

"I wish I had a sister," his friend said, breathless to comfort, "I'd let you go out with her."

The evening was over. The bartender was cashing his tips. They were the last to leave. The fall street was empty. Shops were boarded up, the tourists long gone. The town was theirs again. There was no moon. The cloudy sky was heavy and close, the air sweating with smells—skunk, dead bait, low tide.

"We don't watch out they'll take over everything," Dick said.

"Not many here in the winter at least," the other said. "Bill Barnes, he's okay, and the guy he hangs out with."

"Yeah, they're okay. I don't mind them."

"And the cook at Waldo's, smiley bastard."

"And that big ugly mother, always got a toothpick in his mouth."

"I wouldn't want to tangle with him."

"And then there's Bisqua."

"He's Cape Verdes."

"So's a lot of people."

"Darn good people too."

"Darn right."

"And the old guy in the black suit."

"What's he, some kind of minister?"

"Yeah, what *is* he anyway?"

"He's always been around, but he don't talk to nobody."

"He might be an Indian."

"Yeah?" Dick said. "You think?"

"You never really know."

"I got nothing against Indians."

"Hell, neither do I."

They turned down a narrow, unlit lane, under sagging boughs. Dark houses loomed together, mossy and dank. Something stirred in the privet, and they bumped to a stop, trying to see into the dark. The rustle recurred, stealthy and brief. They grabbed each other's elbow, half crouched.

Between the bushes a bent figure arose to its full height, vibrating with impenitent glee.

Dick drew breath. "It's only Czezarley Zoo."

The oldster held his ground for half an instant more, then his habitual terrors mastered him and he fled back into the leaves.

"Who let you out this time of night, Uncle Chas?" Dick called in a hoarse voice.

They heard clumsy thongs clumping across a soft lawn, then nothing.

"I thought it was a fucking . . . bear," said the other.

"Ought to lock him up."

"Never happen. You know what they say about Uncle Chas."

"No."

"He's related to everybody in town."

Dick gave a snort, and they went on laughing loudly, vigilant in the dark.

The Sandbox

That little boy who thinks he's a girl? Kyle? He's got two mommies, but he's not adopted. He's not even a turkey-baster job. Darlana's his real mother. Her lover Bev says, "One man, one night. Not bad!"

When was five years ago. I never dared ask who.

He had a play date with Jill at my house. They had a problem right from the start. They played Peter Pan. He insisted on being Wendy or Tinker Bell instead of Captain Hook. He wanted the female roles. He came dressed as a ballerina, in pink leotards and a tutu.

They've raised him without any kind of gender identification. It's okay with me, whatever he wants to be. It wasn't my place to tell him otherwise. How his teachers cope I can't imagine.

Finally they got in a real tiff. Over Jill's favorite doll? She's very possessive about this doll. She once said to me—I'd picked it up absentmindedly, she snatched it back—she said, "That's not for grownups, that's for children."

So Kyle began playing with the doll. Jill got very upset. She got really obstreperous, she says, "You're a boy, you can't have a doll."

He said, "I'm a girl."

She says, "No, you're not, you're a boy."

He says, "No, I'm not, I'm a girl."

They went back and forth, getting louder all the while. I said, "Children, children!" All I wanted was to keep the peace.

Right in the middle of this the mommies come to pick him up. Both of them. Darlana hardly ever speaks. She's a nodder, she nods at everything Bev says, but when she does open her mouth it's always to ridicule something the person Bev's talking to has just said, and these strange phrases pop out like, "We won't dignatise that with an answer," or "That beggars the question."

So we're making small talk about the schools here, how backward they are. Meanwhile the fight continues. Jill keeps saying, "That's a girl toy, not a boy toy."

Bev got a little huffy. She corrected Jill, she says, "That's a toy toy. There's no difference between boys and girls."

Then she says to me, "We hate these sexual stereotypes. We don't allow them in our home. Kyle's decided he wants to be a girl. We've talked it over and he prefers to be a girl. If he wants to be a girl he can be a girl. He can be anything he wants to be."

Darlana's nodding and nodding. I found myself nodding too, only in a circle sort of, like a clock. I was getting dizzy. So I tried the other way, counter clockwise. I even heard my neck crack.

Jill says, "Mo-ther!" the way she does.

I'm still nodding away. I'm dazed is the truth. And suddenly Jill has like a paroxysm and starts jumping up and down shouting, "He's a boy, he's a boy, he's a boy."

Bev says, "He can be a girl If he wants to be."

Jill says, "No, he can't." Then she looks at me and says, "Mother," again. Only this time it's like, "Muuh-therrr!"

Bev says in this very deep, professorial voice, "He certainly can. He can follow his dreams. We're not going to put any limits on him."

And Jill yells, she's really exasperated, "He can't either."

Darlana says, "What's goose for the gander's gander for geese. If you can be a girl so can Kyle."

I could feel myself squinting. And Jill yells, "He can't be a girl, he can't he can't he can't, he's got a PEE NUSS."

That sounded like the settler right there. She's always so definite about everything. I wonder where she gets that. I was just trying to jolly them along, walk the line. I didn't want to get into any Lesbian-feminist arguments, so I said in my most moderate, reasonable tone, "Now, we don't know that, Jill."

And Jill just shouts, "Yes, we do too. He's a boy and he's got a PEE NUSS."

I never heard the word so like *loud* before? I don't know. I think their whole lives are about women. He may have got the idea that it's not so good to be a man in this world. I mean I wonder what he'll think when he's grown up.

Bev might be right about dolls though. Well, you have to sympathize. Talk about diversity. This town's on the cutting edge. The new kindergarten teacher decided to have her class produce a global play. Each of the kids would represent a different country and wear the national costume. They drew lots and she sent a letter to the parents asking them to help with the costumes.

You wouldn't believe the turmoil! Esther Morley wanted to know why her son had to portray Sweden. Her husband's black. One time when she was busy he went to pick up Jill at someone's house and brought back another little blond girl. He's so nice, he's always doing things for people. When they were studying the Civil War in school their daughter came home and said, "Mommy, is Daddy a slave?"

Sean Riley drew Africa, but his parents didn't see why he couldn't be Ireland. He's got red hair and freckles and an antique shillelagh.

But Sally Tran Dong—her father runs the Chinese restaurant—had Ireland, though she's fluent in Vietnamese and has a whole closetful of kimonos.

Everybody was in an uproar. Jill got France, which sounds safe, except the teacher wanted her to wear a garter. It just happened to be a very trying day for me and I was the last one to show up at school. When I said I didn't think it proper for a five year old to be doing the cancan on stage in front of the public the teacher broke down in tears. She said, "After all this I can't believe you're complaining about getting France."

You know me, never at a loss. "Well," I says, "I wouldn't mind so much if I hadn't just read they're making us pay rent on our war graves."

Of course everybody thinks their own child is the brightest in the class, much too good to be stuck in with the ordinary little dullards and thugs, and they're all demanding a special teacher for the gifted, or at least that their kid be skipped a grade. Of course none of them can hide that they think their own child is by far the best in every possible way. In fact of course Jill's miles ahead of them all.

The Way Things Are

It turned out I had a fantastic vacation after all. Ordinarily I would've just stayed in town and had a few drinks. I probably would've been too depressed even to get myself out of bed most days. That's just the way it is. What can I say? But I ended up in Honolulu. I had a great time, my first real vacation in years.

You'll never believe how it happened. I had an old friend in New York named Joshua. We go way back, we used to make the rounds every night. The last time I went to see him he said—he wasn't doing very well—he said, "Annie, I've always wanted to go to Hawaii, I'm going to take you, I've got all these frequent flyer miles saved up, but I've never been there, I've always wanted to go there, it's the one place I've never been, and I'm going to take you."

"Yeah, yeah," I said. He kept talking about it, he kept promising. He says, "If I don't do it now I never will."

"So do it," I said. "Go for it."

"I will," he says. "I'm going to. You wait."

I knew he never would. He wasn't really all there half the time. I mean, I knew he would *like* to do it. I would've liked it myself.

He was a completely solitary person. All his old lovers were dead a long time ago. I don't know how he managed. When I got back here I was very worried about him. I'd call him up, he'd start talking about taking me to Hawaii. So I'd humor him, you know, I'd say, "Let's do it, come on, let's do it, it'll be the best fling we ever had."

Poor man, most of the time he hardly even knew where he was anymore. When he died I got a phone call. So I went down to clean out his apartment. The first drawer I opened had two tickets to Honolulu right on top.

So I took Ozzie. He's not doing so great either. His doctor told him to watch out for the sun. Ozzie used to live for the beach, he got burned to a crisp on Waikiki, so now he's in bed with all these suppurating blisters and sores. I had a good time though. Of course it wasn't the same as going with Joshua. But that's just the way things are.

Paint

I don't go to the club but once every couple of years now. I used to go every Saturday night, but I lost the habit. The old-timers are gone. There's no serious artists there anymore, no real talk, just gossip. They don't even drink really. Just beer and wine. They play a lot of ping-pong and pool. Well, they're younger, they don't have much to say.

I moved up here from Pensacola when I retired from the Navy. I was in Tokyo Bay for the surrender. Sixty-three years I was married. My wife died ten years ago, I still miss her. I've got kids, grand-kids, great-grand-kids, scattered all over the world. When I started out in life I never expected that. I didn't know anything about paint either, I never went to school past the eigth grade.

First time I was overseas I fell in love with Cezanne, Monet, Manet, that school. I seen both Theatres. I hate Picasso. He was the end. I don't show my paintings, and I never will. When I've finished something I like I give it to a friend. I'm painting the ponds around here. In all seasons. I like the stillness of ponds. I'm making a statement about vanishing beauty. I've got hundreds of canvases. Twenty-two years' worth. I work like a beaver, but I'm never satisfied. I don't set foot in the galleries. They turn my stomach. The Nothing School of Blotch and Smear. Nobody bothers to learn how to draw. It's all caricature and phony colors now. Nobody knows the difference and nobody understands what I'm saying. So I shut up. Years ago. I just paint from the heart. I'm always happy—most of the time—so maybe I'm one of the good guys.

Last time I went though, it shook me up. It was the middle of winter. There were a lot of new members I'd never met. Fresh-faced kids with all their hair—in their thirties and forties—not a wrinkle among them. And a few old geezers like me. Nigel Smythe was up from Washington for a funeral on Sunday. Sucking on a cigarette like it's a life-support system. Even while he's eating. He's got a permanent squint. He even looks like a newspaperman. I guess he'd rather be called a journalist. A pundit maybe.

Dinner was the usual uproar and insults. You wouldn't want to be a fly on the wall if you were a woman. When the coffee came T'bor stood up and announced that Vankel had died last week in Santa Fe and asked for a minute's silence. You could almost hear people counting down like New Year's Eve, and then everybody beat on the tables with their silverware and made a big hulla-baloo. It wasn't disrespectful, it's a tradition. Nothing's allowed to be serious. Except art. In the old days, I mean.

Afterwards us diehards sat around the fire. Nobody was in a hurry to go home. There was plenty of whiskey. That was like the old days at least. It was a real treat. I live alone. I don't keep a bot-tle at home. I never go out, but I'm not averse to a few belts when there's conversation to be had.

Of course the young folks there had never even heard of Vankel. T'bor said he'd dreaded having to ask for the minute of silence.

Nigel said, "Ten seconds would have been plenty."

T'bor said, "Don't stint the dead."

"Vankel was a lousy sculptor," Nigel says.

"I don't care," T'bor says. "I miss him."

"He was a bore," Nigel says. "He got worse every year."

In my opinion Vankel's trouble was he was impetuous. He al-ways stopped to think too late. And then his health went bad, and then he lost his strength—The End if you're a stone carver. Half the time he was cockeyed at what he wound up with. His pieces never turned out the way he planned. With stone you can only get smaller. He chipped his blocks away to midgets, gargoyles, you might say, like primitives. You wouldn't always have guessed it was a human figure. I remember one day—he was trying to decide if his new monstrosity was done or not. He walks around and around it. It looks like something different from every angle. He's got his hat off and scratching his head, he's up to his ankles in rubble. He says, "What d'you think? It's called *Sea Sprite*."

"Oh," I says, "I like it." I meant the name. I was lucky. It's not always so easy to lie.

"Vankel's been doddering for years," Philly says. "It's a favor to everybody, himself included."

Philly hasn't exactly been in great shape lately. He's terrified of getting senile and being locked away and forgotten. He was an architect. Made a bundle too. Lost it all to lawyers. Handed over his firm to his sons and then sued them when they started doing malls. Spent his last good years in court.

"I liked Vankel," T'bor says. "He was lonely. He used to drink all night at one bar or another. He'd wait until the last patron left, and then he'd walk him home. Man or woman, it didn't matter. Sometimes people got the wrong idea."

"He was a bore," Nigel says. "Johnny One Note. He was like a pit bull with his teeth in one idea."

"Even so I miss him," T'bor says.

Nigel just scoffed, he says, "You haven't given him a thought since he left town."

"Even so," T'bor said. "Now I miss him. Never send to know."

"Ding dong," says Nigel. "Not for me. He was a worthless bore. Why should I pretend I care?"

You could see T'bor wince. He's the soul of forbearance. He's a cartoonist, but he never takes cheap shots. He's morally—I guess you could say—fastidious. He's got a passionate energy, which he keeps under wraps. He's happiest when he doesn't have to use a caption. He says, "But you've got to admit that you feel some-

Paint

thing, some kinship. Maybe against your will. In spite of yourself. But something."

Nigel never concedes anything. He milks his cynicism. He's a bony little gnome in a white shirt—very elegant too—all hunched and shrunk, with a huge bristly head of hair and thick glasses that magnify his squint. He always keeps one elbow on the table, wrist straight out like a pistol, these two long nicotine-stained fingers with an unfiltered butt between them letting off loops of blue smoke like he's just shot some nitwit.

And T'bor never gives up either. In his own way he's even more uncompromising. He always trys to eke the best out of people. He looked sad. He actually sounded plaintive.

Nigel said, "I can honestly say all I feel is a slight sense of relief that I will never again find myself face to face across the dinner table from him."

You could see T'bor flinch. Probably scared the gods might take offense, and include him. He says to Dietrich, "What d'you think?"

Dietrich was a jeweler. A socialist. He never says much anymore. I think he just gave up. He doesn't care about anything now except catching bluefish and stripers for his smokehouse. He says, "I feel sorry for everybody. Alive *or* dead."

Nigel says, "Ten years at most, we'll all be gone. There won't be one of us sitting here. And it won't matter one bit."

Of course he's right about that. Vankel was seventy-five anyway. Well, younger than me. At eighty-eight you can drop dead any minute, but you can't stop to think about it. Even if I started in the crib though I'd still need a thousand years.

"Nooo," Nigel says, "I don't feel bad at all. About anything." And he chains up another smoke and pours himself some more Scotch. "Anyway," he says, "I'm going to be up all night writing Brandon Berrube's eulogy. I'm just getting primed."

Gelby Nelson says, "I don't envy you that."

After Gelby's wife died he grew those grandiose mustachios. Felt free, I guess. Or he uses them for cover. He wrote some novels. Back in the '50s. When I first met him I asked where I could get one. He said they were out of print. I tried the library. Library said they'd all been stolen. So I asked him to loan me one. He said he would, but he never did. I kept asking and he kept promising, and finally I had to think he didn't care. Or did care. Either way I was just as happy. What I like are books about great artists. I'm always amazed though at how many of them got downhearted.

Nigel says, "It's just another job of work."

Gelby said, "I mean, he wrote so many different kinds of things, he mastered so many fields. It won't be easy to do him justice. He was an intellectual industry of one."

T'bor said, "Of course nobody ever saw him. He didn't have much of a life."

"Oh, he had a life, but it wasn't people," Omar McNaut said. "I used to see him. We were contemporaries, more or less. I never knew how he did it. He wrote a book on Egypt. One on the Greeks. One on the Etruscans. One on the Renaissance. He wrote a book about everything."

"And died on his ninety-fifth birthday," Nigel said.

"Birthdays!" Omar said. "I've had enough of those. I don't even take note anymore. I've wiped the date clean out of my mind. I couldn't even tell you when I was born."

"August twelfth, 1893," Philly says.

"Thank you," Omar says. "I didn't hear that."

"1893," Philly shouts.

Omar shakes his head at us. "Can't hear a thing," he says. "Sounds like there's an insect in my ear."

"Invaluable gift," Philly says, "forgetfulness."

I haven't seen Omar in I don't know how long. He's starting to show his age. He sits there holding his cane and takes tiny little sips of his whiskey. His hand shakes. He said he doesn't paint much anymore, he's thankful just to be able to look. But it gave me a turn. He's a very modest person. You can tell his things a mile away, they're always mauve, greyish, dark blues and blacks, sort of muted, dream silhouettes. Dense atmosphere. Like unfocused glimpses at dusk, long vistas, vague shapes in the distance just before you recognize them, like déjà vu. One step forward it's all a blur, one step back nostalgia.

Nigel said, "Brandon got pretty testy toward the end. He said he didn't want to be human."

T'bor said, "What did he mean by that? Didn't want to be mortal?"

"Too good for death," Philly says. "He was a snob. Garden variety."

Nigel said, "I don't think so. That wasn't the way I took it."

Dietrich says, "What he learned from ninety-five years." His accent is coming back more every year. He's built like a barrel. He's even starting to look as if he'd never left Bremerhaven after all.

"Ninety-five years and forty books," Nigel says. "Not to mention posthumous works, yet to come. He'll be around for a while."

"So he didn't want to age," Philly said. "Join the crowd."

"Nooo," Nigel says, "I don't think he meant that either."

T'bor says, "No matter how you twist and turn no one ever gets quit of their guilt."

"If you're a big enough bastard!" Philly says. His volume is starting to go up.

Dietrich said, "I agree with T'bor. Hitler used to make his mistresses squat over his face and shit on him. Which only proves nobody's all bad."

I never heard that about Hitler. I knew he was a vegetarian. I was on a picketboat at Okinawa. Kamikazes and the hammering flak like big black popcorn. I've never been so scared. We had no idea people could act like that. I was glad when they dropped the

Bomb. Now they say it was wrong. I don't hate the Japanese anymore. When they were trying to kill me I did.

Gelby says, "There's no cure for life but death."

Omar says, "And maybe not even that."

And right along in there somewhere I remember—you know
how things happen and nobody takes any notice—the fire started
to hiss and whine, then it began to roar. Really roar. We backed
our chairs up a bit, but the flames never changed. The heat must
have reached a pocket of gas or something. But the fire just stayed
this smooth blue cocoon around the whole log which was glowing
orange-red with little specks of white light winking through like
fireflies. And roaring away inside like a jet plane. It was weird but
nobody mentioned it.

"It's all a matter of timing," T'bor said. "But it's not simple.
Too much responsibility for most people. I like to think that if you
live long enough there's nothing to choose between the two states.
Some people call it crossing over."

"Yeah," Philly says, "but don't jump the gun."

I guess he meant his brother Willis, who was depressed for
years. Philly finally made him take a trip to Mexico. He gave
Willis the money to revisit the scenes that inspired his youth when
he did a series of paintings of the sun. He had a big success in New
York with them, and then he moved up here to be near Philly, and
after that nothing ever panned out for him again. Anyhow, he got
a bug down there and died.

"I respect Brandon's accomplishment," Nigel says. "I didn't
especially like him. He wasn't likeable, not that it signifies. I told
him once that Howard Ainsworth had very much wanted to see
him before he died. They went way back, those two, they were old
friends. And Brandon said, 'Didn't he know I was busy?'"

T'bor says, "Greed exceeds grasp."

"That wasn't it either," Nigel said. "He didn't want to be human at all."

"Better? Beyond pain? Free? An animal? A spirit?" T'bor says, very steady, very quiet, which is about as combative as he gets.

"None of those," Nigel says. "Not. Human. At. All."

T-bor looked at him but he didn't say anything else. I could see him kissing his tongue.

"So," I says, "what're you going to put in this eulogy?"

"Not that," Nigel says. He sits up straight and glares at me, and then he points those two fingers right between my eyes. "I'm not going to write something I don't understand and can't verify. And that's the truth—I simply have no idea what he meant. Maybe I misheard. That's the only thing he ever said in my hearing that didn't make sense."

"Nigel," I says, "I've never heard you talk this way. I thought you had all the keys to everything."

He says, "Over a million words of mine have seen print, and the only thing I can say for sure is, I've never had to eat a single one, and I'm not going to start now."

"Well," Gelby says, "it *would* sound pretty bald all by itself. Like saying you've got a great story but you're not telling it."

Nigel says, "I stick to the verifiable. Providing it leads somewhere. I don't traffic in aberrations. I leave the novels to you."

"I've retired," Gelby said. "They gave me indigestion."

"Lost your nerve," Nigel says. "Or bought into your own mediocrity. Which comes to the same."

All you can see is Gelby's mustachios. He says, "As a matter of fact I wrote a piece on Berrube once, but he wouldn't let me publish it."

"I wonder why not," Omar says. "Let me guess."

"That was the agreement," Gelby says. "We worked on it together. I could never get him to sign off on it."

Omar said, "You may think you're a god but mostly you're just a goddamned fool. He was a magnificent phenomenon, all the same."

"He was just another jerk," Philly roars. "Like the rest of us."

Philly's a wreck. He's the youngest of us too. I don't think he's even seventy yet. Willis was really the only person he was ever close to, including his wife, and he divorced her right after Willis died. He just about self-destructed, turned against every interest of his own, compounded all his mistakes. When things got bad he made them worse. For a while he drank and chased after every skirt that went by. "Young chicks," he'd say. "That's all there is. What else is there?" He was always trying to get me to go tomcatting with him. He wound up in the hospital for his diabetes, and when he came out he was impotent. And then he lost that lawsuit with his sons.

"It's what's left after the life that matters," Nigel says.

Philly says, "Yeah, life's like plans you do for a cathedral and when you look they've put up an outhouse."

T'bor says, "Who's this *they*?"

"Sleepwalkers," says Omar.

"Editors," says Gelby.

Nigel says, "If you'd stayed in New York you'd still be publishing. Berrube only spent one month a year here, out in the dunes by himself, and all he did there was work. P-town's a graveyard for artists and writers. It's too comfortable. It's insidious. The pursuit of happiness is a way of life here. No pain, no art. Time just seeps away. Too much drainage, so to speak."

Omar says, "Being born is pain enough."

"Wrong kind," Nigel says. "There's no solitude here. Ambition's dead. Everybody's all of a level. Scratch my back, I'll scratch yours."

T'bor says, "Some people use a clam rake."

"I know some that favor their teeth," Omar says.

Of course I don't know anything about any of this stuff. I started late. I never lived in New York. I never lived the bohemian life anywhere. I'm just lucky I ever learned there was such a thing as paint. I only wish I'd known it sooner.

Nigel says, "I tell the truth. Why shouldn't I? Vankel was a lousy sculptor. What interests me is, did he know it, and if so, why did he waste his whole life at it? I don't say he wasn't an honest drudge."

"Oh, he knew," Omar says. "He had a great photograph of Dickinson and Hofmann on his wall for years. I happened to come across that same picture somewhere else, and he was on one end of it. He'd just snipped himself off. When I mentioned it to him he claimed it was only because they were painters, and he being a sculptor didn't belong. At least he had some humility."

"He was a disappointed man, I think," T'bor says. "He felt obsolete."

Dietrich gave a little snort of disgust and a nod.

"Maybe that's why he was always so garrulous," Nigel says. "After Ring Lardner lost his inspiration he beat his face to a bloody pulp against the typewriter keys. Personally I don't regret I had no original gift. As apt to be a curse as not."

"Gelby," I says—I don't know what got into me—I says, "Gelby, when are you going to let me read one of your books?"

"Can't," he says. "There aren't anymore. They've all been pulped themselves. No blood there at least. I took mine to the dump. Long since."

"So you don't write anymore?" I says.

Nigel says, "He's become an antiquarian. He tends to the local."

"The particular. The unique. The out of the way. As long as I'm here," Gelby says. "Poetry."

"Fiddle-faddle," Nigel says. "Last resort of the failed fictioneer, hobby of those who renounce success. No fame, no development."

I can see T'bor glooming, but Gelby doesn't blink an eye—I actually think he smiled, you can't always tell with him.

"It's voracity," Nigel says. "Even more important than talent. Some have it. Some don't."

"I gave up once too often," Gelby says. "It got too hard to get started again. I didn't want to write the kinds of things I knew. Once you've used up your youth you've got to be more ruthless. Poetry's abstract. You don't have to shed anybody's blood but your own."

"In my experience," Omar says, "there are cases—rare, I grant—where it's just a matter of play. Nature, if you like. Or second nature. Kimball Tardiff, for example."

"True," Nigel says, "there's Kimball," and he cocks his wrist and squints more than ever. "A complete loner. Just the opposite of Berrube, who was such a stickler for convention, lived in a suit and tie, church every Sunday, faithful family life.

"Tardiff never won any prizes, or anything else. Whenever you ask him how he is, he always says, 'Poor. Poor.' He can hardly sell his stuff at all. It looks too easy, it looks like jokes, pseudoart I once heard someone call it. It's all so different, he's had so many phases, people take offense, and there's also such a lot of it. He can't help himself. He works every day of the year, he's done by nine A.M., and then he drinks until the bars open, and then he takes a nap. He's got the constitution of a clock."

"Another jerk heard from," Philly says.

Philly resents it that nobody thinks of him as an artist. He wrote a couple of books on restoring old houses, but nobody calls *him* a writer. He and Kimball were great pals at one time. Years ago when Kimball's studio filled up with those crazy contraptions he makes out of scraps from the dump, Philly let him put a group of them on his lawn.

That was before I came to town, but I remember them when they were all weathered and falling apart. People would stop and discuss what the devil they were. Each one looked like something, even if you couldn't figure out what. They were completely convincing, made of finished wood, cast-off gadgets and whatnot, very ornamental, finely wrought. He's a relentless craftsman.

There wasn't a rough spot or anything makeshift, and there they were just rotting away on Philly's front lawn, turning black, growing moss, sagging like ruins. For a while a family of skunks lived in one. People were liable to puzzle and puzzle and then suddenly laugh like mad and walk off. I asked him about a certain one once. He said, "Oh, it's a child's sarcophagus."

Philly decided to spruce up his property and had them all carted to the dump. He didn't even bother to tell Kimball, much less ask his permission. That was the end of that friendship. Philly went around saying, "Ashes to ashes, junk to junk,'" and how he should've charged Kimball rent for use of his lawn.

Kimball called Philly a Vandal.

Dietrich said, "Kimball you never see anymore. He was not clubbable. Never did anything but art and drink. Never married, never girlfriends. Never car, never phone. No TV. Never had a thought, that I ever heard. Funny thing though, he loved that old encyclopedia somebody threw out. And he only had the last half. He never bothered to lug the rest of it home. He was missing *A* through *M*, but he didn't care. He was captivated by facts. Any facts. One time he says, '*N* through *Z* is more than enough for me.'"

"I don't envy him *either*," Gelby says.

"Saved by his obsessions," Omar said. "He doesn't seem to age at all He just gets more invisible."

"He's pickled," Philly said. "He's hibernating. Sleep's his real talent."

"You need your rest," T'bor says, "if you do as much as he does."

"Mr. Snooze," Philly says.

Dietrich says to Nigel, "And Vankel's one idea was what?"

"Oh," Nigel says, "he had a new one every time you ran into him. Whatever it was though he was infatuated, and he'd completely forgotten all the others. He had a child's shamelessness.

He was flagrant about everything, he could aggravate you to tears."

I hardly ever talked to Vankel, so I can't vouch. Maybe to Nigel he was just poaching. But once you're retired what's left to do but think? Worst thing that could happen, I guess.

"For instance," Dietrich says. "Give examples."

"Ohhh," Nigel says—he was annoyed—he says, "Vankel wouldn't know an idea if it chopped his head off."

"You can't remember even one?" says Dietrich. "You should have made notes. What kind of reporter you are?"

Nigel says, "Nothing there to report—papier-mâché is the right medium for sculpture because only clothes matter now. Walt Disney precipitated the decline of American civilization. Space probes as acupuncture for God. Puerilities. Meanwhile he went right on mutilating stone."

"Life at hard labor," Philly says. "Might as well have been in Leavenworth."

T'bor's stubborn. He says, "Vankel was a serious man. He has a place in my heart, a stone in my personal graveyard."

"A fool," says Nigel.

"Here's to him, I say," Dietrich said.

"I'll drink to him," Nigel says. "With pleasure."

"Dead or alive, he's still a jerk," Philly said, but he lifted up his glass with the rest of us.

By this time everybody was feeling good but him. He's apt to get meaner till he gets maudlin and then all of a sudden he loves everybody. But that happens later, if it happens at all. He's more likely to fall asleep like Kimball. I remember them leaning together on the same bench, snoring away in unison. Like the wife and I, sad to say.

Thank God at least he doesn't still rave about his invincible erection. He had a pump implanted in his scrotum to cure his diabetic impotence. He used to brag how he could go for hours and thrill the gals to death. By then though he'd grown so vindictive no woman could bear him for five minutes, so then he said all there were in town now was dykes. His little eyes were hard as ball bearings about to explode, not to mention how portly he'd grown, and his boils and his scrofulous eruptions and his gout. He says to me one time, "Just call me Job."

T'bor says—he's always trying to keep the conversation up to a certain level—he says, "I'll tell you a dream I had the other night. I was in a big crowd of people looking up at something way off in the distance. We were all straining our eyes, and then a sort of mountain rose up with a gallows on it, only it turned out to be Jesus Christ on the Cross.

"We were all there waiting for him to speak, but he didn't have a mouth. He had eyes and a nose and ears, and his hands and feet were nailed to the Cross—you could see the bloody spear wound in his side—and he had his crown of thorns, but under his nose all he had was a blank chin. And everybody was waiting for him to speak."

"And you woke up? He never spoke?" Gelby says.

"I was glad to wake up," T'bor says. "I have to admit."

"Sounds right up your alley," Omar says.

"I don't know if I'm ready yet for that one," T'bor says.

Philly says, "I thought you were a Jew."

T'bor says, "I *am* a Jew. Once a Jew always a Jew. Even if you convert. You can't stop being a Jew."

Philly says, "Christ did."

Omar says, "Christ was the quintessential Jew."

"Whatever he started out," Philly says, "whatever he intended, he ended up a Christian."

"According to Nietzsche," Dietrich says, "the only true Christian there ever was."

"One was enough," Gelby says.

Philly says, "Scourge of the Chosen People."

"Chosen to suffer—not to slight the Irish," Omar says. "By The Old Bastard Himself. Who sent His only Son to bring his people woe. More and worse."

"As if the Jews hadn't had enough already," T'bor says.

"Arrogant bastards," Philly said. "The Romans had a lot to put up with."

"It's pretty hard not to despise the Jews," Nigel says, "for spawning Christendom and Islam both."

Even T'bor had to smile at that.

"Man must suffer to be vize," Dietrich sort of intones with his accent. "According to Essheelos." Whoever that is.

"Ass hole us," Philly says.

T'bor says, "I don't have much faith in suffering. It's too late in history for that. It reminds me of when Jake Nathan was dying. He was a great painter, you know. He had a good, long life, full of honors. A retrospective at the Whitney. Everything any artist could ever want. He was surrounded by loving family. He had invested wisely. His children were successful. His grandchildren's future was secure, at least as secure as he could make it. His whole life had been a perfect marvel of good-fortune and public esteem. And he'd earned it too. He had nothing to fear, no reason for remorse. You know how rare that is! All he had to do was get through his dying.

"And there he was on his deathbed—no physical pain—absolutely in despair about Israel. For some reason he thought the end had come, or some awful disaster was in store. All he wanted was to have the *Times* read to him, and watch for bulletins on TV. He was desolate. And there was nothing anyone could do to ease his mind."

"What on earth was going on?" Omar says.

"Four years ago?" T'bor says. "1979? I don't know. Who remembers? One crisis or another."

Philly says, "I'd rather be a fool like Vankel."

"Vankel was a Jew too," T'bor said.

"Too goddamned many Jews," Philly says.

"Another Russian," Omar says. "That's why we won the Cold War. Before it even began."

"I wouldn't give a cup of piss for the whole crock of history," Philly says.

"If we knew everything about the universe, nothing would be different," Nigel says.

Gelby said, "Except no hope."

"Ah, well," Nigel says, "Philly'd still have his legendary love life. Local affairs for Gelby's pen."

"Pump's broke," Philly said.

"Call a plumber," Dietrich says. "Quick! While it's winter and you can still get one."

"No point," Philly says.

"Ah, jaded one," Nigel says, "sick of young chicks, who siftest the grains of beach sand."

"Pump's no use," Philly says, "if the plumbing leaks."

Dietrich says, "Fix the pump and the plumbing will seal itself."

"Too late," Philly says. "I never even got to try it out."

Everybody sat there sort of blank.

Finally Nigel says, "You mean all this time we've envied you in vain?"

Philly just laughed like a shout. Louder and louder he gets the more he drinks. "Hate to disillusion you," he says.

"I guess there never *was* any hope," Gelby says, and he gives a little chuckle.

"So what do you do," Dietrich says, "when you come home tonight and find a young chicken in your bed?"

"Stand her on her head," Philly says, "and drop it in."

"Ah," Omar says with a big brogue, "you're a lucky man. You're on the road to a tranquil sunset, after all."

"Like the rest of you?" Philly says. "I'd rather be dead."

In vino veritas, I guess. I used to like the back and forth, but this just reminded me of all the friends of mine that died young. It's hard to grasp how much they've missed. The future is never what you expect. They'd be amazed. Especially a couple of them that committed suicide. If only they'd held out, everything might have changed. I've never understood suicide. Maybe I'm too happy. All I ask is to go on painting. I miss my wife though. If I live long enough maybe I'll take up portraits. If I ever get done with ponds.

"Somebody's got to keep Nigel in copy," Gelby says. "Besides the late illustrious."

"Philly's yours," Nigel says.

"Not good enough for you, eh?" Philly sneers.

"Bathos," Nigel says. "Fit for maggots."

I don't remember Nigel being so sour. Maybe politics is getting to him. When I asked him how Washington was, he said, "Reagan's trough. You cannot even conceive. Believe me. You're lucky not to know."

"Save your insults," Philly says to Nigel. "I'm leaving a fat bequest for a funeral banquet. I'm counting on you all to piss all over my good name."

"You'll be there," T'bor said. "We'll make a great occasion."

"Get out your notebook, I'll give you my obit," Philly says to Nigel, or maybe Gelby. "Born a jerk, married a jerk, fathered two jerks, tried to fuck some jerks, drank with jerks, died a jerk."

Everybody rolled their eyes. He half means it, and he's half proud of his wrongheadedness. He looks terrible too, all mottled and gasping like a fish. At least ten years the youngest of us. He'll be the first to go, and he knows it. I don't think he ever got anything he really wanted. He had too many appetites. He wanted things to be important, but he could never believe they were, not even his own miseries.

Nigel says to Gelby, "Maybe you'd like to say a word at Brandon's memorial service. That piece of yours needn't go to waste after all. You can have the last laugh."

"No thanks," Gelby said. "I have no quarrel with Brandon Berrube."

Philly yells, "What's the matter? You afraid he'll hear? Come back and haunt you?"

"You think they can hear?" Dietrich breaks in, very serious. "Suppose the dead stay around. Forever, I mean. More and more of them all the time. I used to think about that when I was young. Breathing dead spirits everywhere you go. You would be taken over. You would have no will of your own."

"That's about it," Nigel says. "At least in the provinces."

"You never know," Omar says.

"I hope not," Gelby says. "I'm looking forward to a little privacy."

"That's the first thing you lose when you die," T'bor says.

"No fear," Nigel says. "Brandon's ashes were scattered down in Chevy Chase. I was there. This is just a local show for peons like Gelby."

Gelby says, "I'll be interested to hear what you have to say."

"Of the dead," Omar says, "speak no ill."

"Amend that," Gelby says. "Of the lately dead. After a year everybody's fair game."

"I'll tell you something, "Nigel says, "in confidence. Death means nothing anymore."

"Never did," Omar says.

"Now where've I heard that before?" T'bor says.

Nigel says, "Won't even be cemeteries. Just names on microfiche."

"In that case, while we still can," T'bor says, lifting his glass, "To our friend Vankel!" He never lets go. He never gives up, even when he's won.

Everybody takes a little nip except Nigel who shrugs like he's had a long day, lifts his glass about an inch, puts it down, closes his eyes, sighs and jumps his eyebrows. "Once was enough," he says.

"That's right," T'bor allows. "You already did." And he puts his hand very lightly on Nigel's shoulder, and lifts it away with a flourish like it's a hat dropping a rabbit.

"And never think ill of the living," Philly says. "Unless they piss on you. Bad aim is the one unforgivable sin."

Even Philly was starting to feel good. He loves everybody to tears actually, and hates himself for it. It was only ten o'clock. I was amazed. It felt like four A.M. One of the new members joined us for a minute, just as we were breaking up. Young guy. He looked like a left-over hippie—long ponytail, tall as a tree. He happened to be the cook that night.

I says, "That was the best meal I ever had here." It was too.

Nigel begged to differ. "I've done better myself," he says, "and my recipes are considered fecal by veterans of this ridiculous cult."

"We always thought Vankel was a vile cook," Omar says, completely kind and sweet, "but this beat his worst by a mile."

"Very good, very good," T'bor says to the guy. "Things are looking up."

"Worst pissing pasta I ever had. What're you, a faggot?" Philly said. He was trying to get into his coat, but it was all tangled up. The guy tried to help him. He's very polite, he's doing his best to figure out how he's supposed to act. They're lurching back and forth, Philly's cursing away.

Finally the guy realizes the coat's going on wrong. Philly's bound and determined to get it on inside out and backwards, he's reeling around and swearing at the poor guy who's actually keeping him on his feet at the same time he's trying to get his arms in the right sleeves. Finally he persuades Philly to take it off and start again—and after a whole long rigamarole the guy gets it on him and starts trying to button it up, and then Philly notices it's not his coat.

Philly seized the opportunity, he really outdid himself. He might not be able to stand up but he can still shout. So the guy starts helping him rummage through the pile of coats for the right one, and Philly's roaring at him so mean and savage the poor guy finally begins to think it might not really be a joke after all, and he backs off, shrugs at us, bows to Philly and goes back to the other room. You can hear the ping pong ball in there going pock pock pock.

Philly looks absolutely bereft, like he's lost his last friend. So he pulls all the coats off the bench, sits down in the middle of the pile against the wall, lets out a big sigh and starts snoring.

"Well," T'bor says, "I guess I'll go home and see if I can think of anything funny."

"Not always so easy," Dietrich says.

"No, it isn't," T'bor says, pulling his coat out of the pile. "People don't realize."

We gave Philly up. We left him there. What else could we do? One by one we got our coats and toddled off very slowly like we were walking on ice, which, thank god, we weren't, and next I remember I was all alone down on the beach and the moon was high, one of those perfectly still, bright nights—once in a while you hear a gull yelp and nothing else.

I got up next morning. It was raining. I didn't feel like working indoors with no light. I started going through all my old paintings. I have nothing to be ashamed of. I said, "Darn it, I'm going to die happy. One way or another."

Then I remembered that damn funeral. I never even heard of Brandon Berrube before. I didn't want to listen to any eulogy either. Even if Nigel did stay up all night to write it. But I went anyway. I had to go. Don't ask me why.

There were lots of people there—I haven't been to the Art Association in years—people I'd never seen before, well-to-do people, I guess, dressed-up, dignified types. Cashmere and flannel. Neckties even. Nigel's talk was one of three. He was very impressive. I was surprised. He kept his word too. He never said anything about Berrube not wanting to be human. It was really only a sketch of his career, and a list of his honors.

The other two speakers were more like old friends and took some little digs. They got some chuckles, Nigel never tried. It wasn't like anything I've ever seen. No solemnities. All affable, matter of fact. People standing around. Talking about themselves mostly. Some wine and a huge antipasto off to one side. But I wasn't hungry, and I never drink two days in a row.

Gelby was the only other one of the club there. Afterwards he went up and shook Nigel's hand. I wondered what they were saying, but I left right away. Now I don't even know anymore what I think myself. I spent the rest of the day sitting at my window, watching it rain. I was glad I went though. I don't get out enough. I should get out more. I'm glad I don't.

Tabletalk

I have to go to all these damn dinners with my husband the Mover & Shaker Nonpareil. This one happened to be at the Rotarians. I sat beside a Baptist minister from up-Cape. He's not a bit slim. Red face, bright white hair, bluest eyes you ever saw. I thought he was going to pop out of his shirt. He started right in on transubstantiation.

I said I didn't want to talk about religion because people always got upset. I know because the last time I had a discussion about religion my father swallowed a bean the wrong way and my husband had to give him the Heimlich maneuver.

"Oh," he said, "not to worry. I'm from a thinking religion," and then in the next sentence he began to evangelize me on the new wave of fundamentalism and say condescending things about Catholic dogma. I thought maybe he was baiting me. And then he said the Jews were to be pitied, not persecuted.

Right away I began to get irate. I said, "So what you're saying is the Jews can't get into Heaven."

"Well!" he said. "There's no question of that. The Bible is quite specific on *that* point."

So I said, "It's not that I don't believe in an afterlife, I do. I believe in something, I don't know what exactly. Some power or sense or something."

I usually accept what the priest says, not on abortion of course. Nobody agrees with that except the Pope.

He said, "Aren't you a Christian?"

I said, "Yes, I am, as a matter of fact. But I don't believe in Hell. I don't believe in Heaven either, but if I did the Jews would be the first ones there because they have a covenant with God."

All the while he's eating away. Every time he tried to say something I'd just override him—I was really on a roll—and anyway he was just shoveling the food in. His mouth was always full, all this chicken goop on rice and sticky little peas. It wasn't really edible.

I says, "But I do think we all go somewhere, but it's not Heaven and it's not Hell, but we're all there together, all of us, even Adolph Hitler. I don't know if we'll recognize each other."

That was about the third time he tried to say something. He was really red. I even noticed it. I didn't give him a chance to swallow. I says, "And anyway I don't really consider fundamentalists to be Christians at all."

All of a sudden he says, "I'm losing my vision."

I didn't know what he meant. I thought maybe he was conceding the argument or having a reverse revelation or something.

Then he kept saying, "I'm losing my vision, I'm losing my vision." He was white as a ghost. Everybody gathered round, fanning him, giving him water.

I didn't know it, but he'd had a stroke the year before and going blind is one of the symptoms.

After he got his eyesight back and began to act normal again I said, "I don't think you should drive all the way back up-Cape tonight. You can stay at our house, and we can discuss this some more."

He said, "I'm sure I can find a bed somewhere else in this town."

I kept insisting he come home with us. I kept saying what a comfortable spare room we had, and how fascinated I was by our discussion, and how interested I was in everything he had to say.

He started to get red all over again, and I decided that was probably enough religion for one night.

When we got home my husband said, "Did you find Reverend Munston interesting? You looked quite animated."

"Oh, yes," I said. "I was. Very. He was worth the price of admission."

My husband wasn't really paying attention, he was sitting on the bed, pulling off his shoes and socks. He said, "That didn't cost us anything."

I said, "That's what I meant."

All These Years

I'd never thought of Odette as a painter, or never really quite took it in. Maybe to my acquisitive eye she looked unapt to reward acquaintance with her work, and the fact is I've never seen it anywhere, or if I have I didn't know it was hers.

Actually all I knew about her—well, the reason she even entered my mind was, I happened to be passing her house, taking a street I seldom use, to avoid a person with whom I'd lately had some awkwardness, and I caught a glimpse between her curtains of a crowded wall of drawings, studies for larger things they looked to be, and then I remembered somehow that she lived there. You know how you know such things without knowing just how.

I can tell it's a little one-room place with a sleeping loft, claustrophobic in winter no doubt, cozy too, year-round at least, cheap and full of charm. She's been here forever, managed the same shop for thirty years, came to town about the same time I did, lives alone in every sense, a solitary, apparently without compatriots, and yet she's very nice, smart, articulate, etc.

The last time I saw her—in a way the only time I ever saw her, at least to speak to—was down on the beach a year, two, maybe three years ago. She was sitting on a bulkhead near the old ice house, waiting for the red moonrise, and I stopped for a minute.

She'd just had a show—though I hadn't known it—and sold three paintings which gave her a little pleasure and eased her finances a bit.

I really knew nothing about her, so I asked and she told the tale of her life: born of French in Turin, married in Paris, moved to Quebec, divorce and hard times in New York.

She'd never wanted very much, except to escape brute cities and their misery, not to have to work too hard at jobs she hated, and pay high rent and own a car and lock her doors. All she ever wanted was to paint.

I had to admire her grave enthusiasm and calm demeanor. "It's beautiful," she said, "so beautiful. We're lucky to be here."

It wasn't warm—end of August, hinge of the season. She bent forward, hugging her knees, holding her head up, eyes on the dark horizon. The moon kept not coming up. I was impatient to resume my thoughts and took leave and walked on and before I looked again it was half way up the sky and everything was bathed in light, but I missed the early red.

I remember her now, comely enough, austere and neat, but before her face had acquired its marks of intensity, her life its confidence. I suppose I'd better go see her show.

Who knows if we'll ever speak again, immigrants that we are, *washashores* in the native parlance, lacking mutual friends or family ties, demographic bits without specific gravity, flotsam and jetsam of this backwater, and who would wish it otherwise?

I'll keep seeing her on the street. We'll smile and nod hello. She must be about my age. When she dies I'll go to her funeral, if I'm still alive and hear in time.

God knows who else will be there, or for that matter who'll be at mine.

The Spiritus Step

Right now I'm a wreck of nerves.

I've got all this lube and an hour and a half to kill.

The phone gives these little mini-rings all the time now, but there's never anybody there.

He's got a nice asshole, he's got a really nice asshole, I mean he's got a really, really nice asshole.

He's been dreaming other people's deaths, and so far he's never been wrong. He's afraid to go to sleep any more.

Well, I hate to say it, but I'm going to have as much fun as I possibly can.

The cook died so there's no more gumbo.

So we hired a gay construction crew and a gay landscaper and a gay painter, and of course we assumed everything would get done on time.

After what I saw happen to Bobby and Philip and Little Arthur I don't even want to be alive anymore.

Where can we go to get laid?

At this time of day? Everybody's at the beach.

We could go over to Mungar and Jed's. They never leave the house.

Why should they? They always have good drugs.

Mungar's a jerk, but I hear he's got a humongous dong.

I guess I could get used to that.
What time are we expected for
dinner?

Don't worry. We'll say we're on
a tight schedule.

He's so sick. He's had everything. He says it's like *The
Inferno*. He must have
committed every sin in the
book.

Who? When? Where?
What does it matter?
It came from some
monkey in Zaire.

It was all so
fucked I just
threw a rock at
the nearest
star and
went home
alone.

I died.

It saved my life. I was such a mess for the last twenty-five years
half the time I couldn't have told you where I was, here or Key
West.

I was on one of my week-long binges, and I had a seizure, luck-
iest thing that ever happened to me. D.O.A. They jump-started
me at the hospital.

I've recovered completely. I'm a new man. When I came to it
was so quiet I could actually hear my own voice begging me to
save myself.

I quit drinking, I quit drugs, I changed my whole life-style. I
was so grateful to be alive. I thought all my troubles were over.

Then I found out I'd tested positive for HIV. I saw it in my folder. No one ever told me. I realized I'd been tested without my consent.

I was devastated. At first I considered a lawsuit, then I figured it wouldn't be worth the stress. I never questioned the diagnosis. It might have been a clerical error or somebody else's blood, or just plain wrong, who knows?

Either way, thinking I was HIV turned out to be the second biggest blessing of my life. I began to read about spirituality and I realized I had to take responsibility for creating my own reality.

I learned so much I lost all my fear. I still haven't verified my diagnosis, but I've decided how to live my life with or without AIDS. I've never had any symptoms, but that's not the point. I've had death, and I've had death in my face, and I've handled them both.

So if AIDS is going to take me I'm ready to go. The more I understand about love the more I realize that AIDS for me is the result of self-neglect. And medication wouldn't help.

What needed change was me, not the AIDS. All you are is what you think. That's all anyone is. You can become what you think. I mean, you will anyway, so you'd better choose.

Drugs

I used to do drugs. I mean a lot of drugs. Every drug in the book. All day long, year in, year out. I lived on pills, ups, downs, sleepers, amphetamines, you name it. One day I says, "Yuck, I'm not going to do this anymore." And I quit every last one of them, I never had another snort, another toke, another pill—no more nothin, honey, except of course alcohol and tobacco, and they were enough, they were plenty. And then some!

That was fifteen years ago. I never broke down once the whole time. To tell you the truth I'd had it with drugs.

Now I take thirty-two pills a day. By the handfuls. Morning, noon and night. I have to set my alarm. I'd really like to know how many pills I've taken in the last three, four years. And now no wine, no cigarettes, no coffee.

Sometimes I get a little . . . you know. I think, Hey, I'm sick of this stuff. Some mornings I wake up, I'm tired, I just wish this was over and done with. Just the thought of all the pills I have to take. Not to mention the effort to eat.

Well, it just goes to show, you never know.

February Truth

et lost strange angel, though it's true, we'd all love to stoop to you, lick your tantalizing legs—stripped of those net stockings—from ticklish instep up calf and inner thigh to dew-beaded mons, plump vulva swollen slick, touch tongue tip to clit, then twist your ostentatious tits' nipples stiffened by that slithery, silk camisole, and last, or next to last, lifting you toward a fitting apotheosis, clasp your succulent buttocks so ecstatically clung to by that skin-tight miniskirt, which even drew a nod of rueful tribute, almost umbrage, from the grudging, hard-eyed bouncer, who reigns here, if anybody does, whose perks include free booze and first pick of the garbage, the wronged out to get even, the venturesome, the strayed, the passing through, the balmy, the tipsy, the ingenue.

Precocious bitch, you've kept us guessing: of the guys at the backgammon table you've been giving that whole-throated laugh to, which will have the luck of your quiff tonight, or will it be all three?

And who would scruple at the face, already writ with the coarse compliances of a barfly's life, bent of a girl's sumptuous body, a little pulverized beneath the eyes by doings we are lean from dreams of?

One night with you might be enough, or even half an hour, for who among us bitter-enders long wed to lone obsession, oblivion or solitude itself can picture a minute spent with you except in sexual congress?

Last call comes early this slow night. The bartender's been yawning for an hour. You need nothing more, and though your beaus could use another round they stand and shrug, clustered, a little dour. You lead like a queen. All the purpose of the night follows them following your proud derrière to the door, and dies in the cold air as you disappear.

Hunched along the bar, four sets of lungs deflate and eyelids droop while each tries to decide what to do—go home or have one last consoler for the road, then on to fitful onanism's doze or restless dreamer's desk.

The bartender's bellicose, bland gaze goes mildly round, mocks each of us in turn, who never spoke the whole night long nor met each other's eyes, but now freely marvel, shake heads, purse lips in silent whistle, commune through the bartender's final, all-conceding jump of the eyebrows, his cryptic bow of farewell to your wake, you who took no note of us, but simply took some other men and went, though it is true, if beckoned, if called, if offered—singly, of course—we'd go, we would, we surely would, in dead February at least, I guess, I hope, I fear, I doubt.

Theatre of the Real

I t's a kind of theatre. It's also perfectly serious. And I don't quite know how it happened, but I've become the audience. Of one. The price of admission is pretty steep, and once you're in apparently there's no exit till the final curtain. For which I'm now waiting. With mixed emotions. And a relatively clear conscience. Resigned, is more what I mean. I can't exactly say I'm fond of the lead, though I've come to respect his performance, if not his motives. It's mostly my part that concerns me.

I suppose this all sounds pretty obscure. To be brief, there's this guy at WOMR who's drinking himself to death, with the assistance of various drugs, pills, everything available, the whole menu. He's on a suicide trip. He even talks about it on his show. Nobody believes him anymore, if they ever did. Anyway, no one seems to care.

He's not downcast. He's like an evangelist. He says his life's not worth living and he's vowed to put an end to it. He's going to go out happy. *He* says. And people just think it's a gimmick to get attention, or at least they pretend that's what they think. I'm beginning to suspect everyone else is part of the play too. They're like a chorus of silence.

How I got involved I do not know. I'm not your inveterate good Samaritan. I don't go around befriending people, especially gay people. I just don't happen to belong to that scene. But he drinks in the Old Colony sometimes. I'd see him in the Thrift Shop browsing for books, we got acquainted.

Somewhere along the line he began bragging very personally to

Theatre of the Real

me about killing himself. I didn't think much about it at first. But he was getting blotto all the time. I helped him home a couple of nights. Eventually I began to suggest he cool it a little. I even suggested he join AA or get a prescription for Antabuse or take a week off and go into detox.

He got quite insulted. He said, "I don't think you understand."

I said, "I understand you've got a drinking problem."

"Coming from you," he said.

I said, "But I'm not flirting with suicide."

He said, "This is true love. Love everlasting."

So. One day he finally did it. Only his downstairs neighbor happened to go up and find him passed out in his bed with empty sleeping pill containers and a bottle of Scotch. Black Label. I guess he meant it about going first class.

The rescue squad came and they revived him. He swore at them, and cursed her too. Called her a "fucking busybody."

Now he's back to his old routine, same old repertoire. Except now I'm his only friend. How that happened I do not know. All I know is I'm embroiled in this endless debate about his rationale for killing himself. It's not easy, finding a new rebuttal every day. I'm getting exhausted, I'd like to leave town for a while, take a rest, but I can't. I'd feel too guilty if I came back and he'd managed to get himself dead.

And there doesn't seem to be any help anywhere else either, not that he'd accept any. Everybody else has long since just washed their hands and walked off. Nobody wants to get tainted. There's only me. I actually think he likes it this way. He's terrifically proud of himself, he takes it as a challenge. Not only is he going to succeed at suicide, but he's going to enlist me in the project. He talks about what a good friend I am, but I'm beginning to wonder if he doesn't hate me. It's a little sinister in a way.

I went to the priest. I'm not a Catholic myself. The guy's long lapsed, doesn't believe in God, doesn't believe in anything. Except euthanasia. And only for himself apparently. He doesn't claim it would solve anyone else's problems. Not even mine.

The priest said he couldn't do anything. But he's not letting me off the hook. He said he'd talk to the guy if I brought him over, which of course I cannot do. But he won't intervene on his own. The police said they have no grounds for doing anything. The priest said I shouldn't give up. He said I was morally bound. He's probably right. I can't speak for him or the Church.

So I'm in this perpetual quandary. I can hardly sleep at night. I feel half the town is watching to see who's going to win. Of course I can never escape, I can never be vindicated unless or until he dies a natural death. Or I die first. Or he shuts up. Which he's definitely not going to do. It's become his life's work. It's like a bad marriage in a country with no divorce. I'm starting to pray for cancer or lightning or AIDS, God help him.

Anyway I keep trying. What choice do I have? I say, Why? Tell me again why you're so bent on suicide. You even say you're not all that miserable. You're obviously not out of control. You're enjoying this."

He says—he's a master sophist, he's both deadly serious and completely insincere, he can always devise more reasons to die than I can to keep him alive—the last thing he said was, "Because I'm alone."

I said, "Well, I'm alone. A lot of people are alone."

He said, "You're not alone. You don't know what alone is."

I said, "I don't even remember the last time I got laid. That's how much it meant to me. And frankly I won't be suprised if it never happens again."

He said, "That's not the kind of alone I'm talking about."

I said, "In that case everybody's alone. Let's not get philosophical."

He said, "But not everybody knows it. And not everybody cares. And I myself want out."

"That's very selfish," I said.

He said, "That's all there is. Oneself."

I said, "Don't you have a family?"

He said, "You're my family and I'm saying goodbye. Sayonara. Adios."

And that's it. Day in day out. I'm used to it. When I don't see him around I leave these long convoluted messages on his answering machine. I can't seem to give up. It wouldn't feel right. I'm doing it as much for myself as for him. More. I don't want to have to suffer if the guy dies. I don't even like him. I'm really just doing it for myself. I'm really just covering my ass, so to speak.

At Least

I'll say this at least—sometimes things work out, maybe not all the way, but sort of. I was actually born up-Cape. In a small town, everybody knowing everybody's business. I couldn't take it. You know.

I moved to New York when I was nineteen. I fell in love with all these women. It was the late '60s. I went wild. You can imagine.

I made one friend, one really solid friend for life. He was a male, he did hair, massage, manicure, makeup, everything. He was very good looking, very pretty, he had a lot of style.

We got a place, we lived together three, four years, we came out together. He even went home with me one time. My mother thought we were lovers, we slept in the same bed. Well, it made her happy.

We came to P-town together. Summer of '75. We had a little cabin up in the woods back of Bradford. It was cheap in those days, very romantic. Dank too. It got a little hectic sometimes. All my chicks and his tricks tripping over each other in the dark, it was only one room.

He was a waiter and a dishwasher and a chambermaid and a houseboy, bartender, maître d', he had a million jobs. Things were always going out of business or changing. He couldn't do retail, he was too snippy. He loved to be snide.

I got my own place after a while. I was gardening, working in leather shops, making vests and purses and stuff out of scraps on the side.

He got bored. He couldn't make enough money here. He went back to New York. Maybe '83, or '4. I never saw him again. We used to write, we'd talk on the phone. Then he went to Florida. He moved around a lot down there too, and I sort of lost touch with him.

I'd like to know where the time goes. I'd sell tickets. I'd make a fortune. I guess nobody'd buy though.

Anyway, a couple of years ago I began to obsess about him. I couldn't get him off my mind. It made me so sad. I didn't even have an address. I wrote c/o his parents. He never wrote back.

Every month or so I'd write him another letter. I wasn't going to give up. I figured they were getting forwarded because they never came back. I thought maybe he was in prison and didn't want anybody to know. I couldn't imagine what he might have done. Said the wrong thing to somebody. You can go to jail for that. I know some that did.

I couldn't believe he was mad at me. I knew something was wrong. I should've known. One day he called me up. Of course he had AIDS. He didn't want me to know, he didn't want to upset me. He wasn't going to tell me at all, ever, but I guess my letters finally got to him.

I says, "I'm coming right down, darlin. You should've told me. I can't wait to see you."

He says, "I don't like you to see me this way."

"Darlin," I says, "I know what you look like. On the inside."

"Well," he says, "just so long as you know I'm a mess."

"Without a dress," I says. That was always our old joke.

When I hung up, that's when it really hit me, how tired he sounded. I was determined to go see him in Florida, I was going to nurse him. But it was the middle of summer, I couldn't leave yet. Meanwhile I was saving my pennies. I got all his friends together and we made a tape reminiscing about old times and how much we loved him—we even sang some of his favorite songs, he must have had a good laugh at that—and I sent it down to him.

He called up one last time. He wanted me to thank everybody.

He said it made him very happy. So at least he had that. I was very busy, I was really run ragged. The next time I called he'd gone to a hospice. When I called there he'd just died.

The Losers

I drove out to Bayberry to get some garden supplies. The owner's such a nice lady, she always insists on trundling the cart full of bags of manure.

I opened the trunk—I'd forgotten—it was full of rejected manuscripts, about five hundred or so. They started out in piles, but by that time they were spread over the bottom of the whole trunk about two feet deep.

She gave a gasp like she'd come on a massacre, all these hacked off limbs and joints, hanks of hair, these poor strewn pages all askew, bent paper clips, names and addresses. All sprawled out there, little black alphabets on white fields in neat little rows like tiny tombstones.

I began to apologize. I know she'd never dreamt of such a thing. I said, "They've all been read, these are just the losers."

"It *is* sort of shocking," she said.

I could see her trying to take it in. I kept saying, "They all got read, very carefully by a very conscientious jury. These are just for recycling."

She looked absolutely horrified. She didn't know what to do, call the police, try to make room for the manure, or what. Of course there was no room. It was solid manuscripts, all the way to the back.

I could only roll my eyes and shrug, and finally she started slinging the bags of manure on top. They're all muck-smeared and wet. It was gruesome.

She says, "Most people just use newspapers."

I didn't know what to say. She thinks I'm this nice motherly housewife. When I drove off I looked in the mirror and saw her half turning around sort of surreptitiously to watch.

It is, I know, it's horrible. It makes me sick when I think of it. Believe me. But it's good to be reminded once in a while.

Ghosts

I saw a ghost a moment ago. Manny who's dead drove by, leaning back in his stately way, hands at three and nine on the wheel, hat flat on his head, unfazed and tanned, like he'd been in Florida, not a day past 80, no worse for wear.

He worked in the liquor store back in my drinking days. I always wondered what became of my street-life friends, those bored desperadoes of nihilism, who faded with the times and disappeared without goodbyes, so when I saw his obituary I sent some flowers to the funeral home, and felt nostalgic and sad, like a ghost myself.

That was a year ago. Now here he is driving down Commercial Street about two miles an hour like he always did in that foot-long Oldsmobile of his, still bald as an olive, suave, conspiratorial, fey as ever, and me too sober even to wave.

For a minute there it seemed like a dream, then the real Manny's clown face jumped up at me like a jack in the box.

I'd forgotten who was who, mixed him up, a much younger man, always wise-cracking, all winks and grimaces, the other one, partners they were, dolors of doses of better or worse, adepts both at vicarious hope, one by day, and one by night, but which worked when, who could you ask?

There were two, Manny who died, and the one who didn't, the older guy who just drove by, whose wife—if he has one—wasn't the widow who wrote to me, "Manny had so many friends we never met. Thanks from his family."

Those days I didn't believe in the future, didn't care if I lived or died, wouldn't have wondered if either man was married or had children or was single and only wanted to retire some day and sit in the sun. I didn't figure I'd be around long, and I didn't worry either. I had nothing to lose.

Odd to think, I never saw them together, never even saw them change shifts. The elder always drove alone like an imperturbable totem, a different breed in a different world from his hot-footing, herky-jerky junior of jokes and gesticulation, madcap Manny, a puppet on too many strings, black-eyed Manny, who's the one in the cemetary.

Wasted days, nights of wreckage, dawns of rue, with me criss-crossing their threshhold for want of use and ease of doubt, all I knew was that one name, and laid it on them both.

Fifteen years a family man, I do everything I'm supposed to do, never miss a day of work, or church, though I don't believe, never miss a payment, never miss dinner with my wife and kids, clean work-clothes twice a week, every tool kept sharp in its place—but now, right this minute, how I'd love to go get drunk, taste whiskey, steep in beer, leave tears unwiped to blur my eyes, slap some stranger on the back, nod and shake my head, agree with everybody at the bar on every subject that comes up, be one of the guys again, for a little while be free of all things single and diminishing, stay long enough, sink deep enough, to feel the grievous grandeur of mortality, the boundless democracy of our secret, unconditional lives.

The Present

Time had buried my desire for Anna Androvna. I seldom saw her at all after the death of her second husband, a rich outdoorsman whom painful age had invalided. He did not care for books or drinking or talk of art, or any of the other sedentary pursuits that engrossed her circle, and when his legs finally failed completely he crawled to the beach one December noon and shot himself, and the tide carried him out.

He left a resolute apology, full of wry condolences and fervent good wishes. I often imagined her, sustaining irreconcilable hopes, making her way in neither haste nor hesitation along their favorite path around the frozen pond, through the bare locust grove, following the furrows of his dragging toes, up the grey, bayberry-covered hill to the cliff overlooking the ocean, and finding, as he had intended, no sign of him, not even his pistol.

Her first husband, a prolific, frenzied, talentless poet, had died drunk in London, maddened by his lack of acclaim and convinced of his place among the immortals. He had gathered a little society of disciples whom he lectured on his system of knowledge and who printed a posthumous book of his last maunderings, but she had hardly opened it, and it sat on her shelf for years, with a slightly-insulting letter yellowing inside. Only I, that I know of, on this side of the Atlantic, ever read the book cover to cover.

She had had other men as well, though none for long, and each—to tell the truth—eventually had met one end or another. She outlived them all, and was seventy-five the last time I ran into her.

"What are you doing in town?" I said.

"How are you?" she said.

"Never worse," I said. "It's all over with me."

"But you always say that," she said, and laid her bony fingers on my wrist.

Luckily we were near the Odd Corner, with its oilcloth-covered table in a nook amongst the back shelves of seldom called-for esoterica, where you can nurse a cup of coffee, and never meet a soul.

I was chagrined by the progress of age. She was much more bent and her lined face was splotched from her solitary nights of vodka. She wore galoshes, who had always avoided rainwear, though it was a dry day. Still, I was inspirited to see her.

"Now tell me," I said, "how you happened to marry Leopold the poet. Was it youthful folly? Was he divinely handsome? Or were you only lonely?"

She inspected me sharply. "What have you been doing with yourself?"

"Lucky Leopold," I said. "I'd gladly trade shoes with him."

"Oh, what *is* the matter?" she said, and I heard her bored vexation.

"Life reveals too little. Art demands too much. Nothing means anything," I said, "unless I hear the true story of your weakness for Leopold the poet."

"Then you must have courage," she said with cheerful finality in her musical voice, rolling her Russian *r*s. Like so many émigrés she spoke exquisite English.

Vindictive bravado possessed me. "At least you must tell me why you would never come to bed."

"I never wanted to enough," she said.

"Ah," I said," I was mad for you."

"No, you weren't," she said, "or I might have had you."

I ground my teeth, but I hardly knew what to regret. I tried to relive the night twenty years before that we stood kissing on her doorstep. Those were the days of my *Mole Tales*, dank according to one critic, and now, skimming the book with my mind's eye, it seemed only an onerous waste of effort and loss of life, though that night, making my disappointed way home alone beneath a mocking moon, but still envisioning the proud shelf of my future works, I consoled myself by reflecting that I was lucky to have escaped her powers. Better men than me have been undone by a single night, and never were happy or whole again.

"I could tell you about Celia," she said with an air of concession, "since I just got a letter from her. It's quite wonderful how lives can work out in the end. For some people. It makes one happy, as if one had something to do with it.

"Anyway, she was the first friend I made in America, when we were both twenty-nine. She painted some good pictures finally, but that was long, long after.

"In those days she was living with an older man, a sort of guru named Ledlie Harward, a retired psychiatrist, handsome and engaging in a grizzled way, and a person with a reason for everything he did. He always claimed he had never made a mistake in his life. He had inherited some money, and she in order to keep her independence held various jobs—they moved around a lot—but she would have died if he had told her to. He had lovers but she was not allowed, and this caused certain problems at times, which she struggled with more or less successfully, depending on how infatuated he got and how often he brought them home. He had ideas about what was natural, and she accepted them, advocated them, I should say, and they had their periods of happiness and misery like the rest of us. She was quite the wilder of the two. He was what is now called mellow, and nothing perturbed him.

"She loved tropical fish and their living room was walled with aquariums and mirrors, which she liked to dance in front of in the afternoon when Ledlie was out. I'll never forget the kaleidoscope of moving fish around her in the shafts of sunlight. She was a fantastic figure with her short red hair, and when she danced the gnarled expression went out of her face. I might add that she was absolutely chaste though everyone was after her.

"She couldn't think what to get Ledlie for his fiftieth birthday. She thought about it quite a lot and finally she decided that what he would like most would be a woman. One by one she considered her attractive friends, but he had had them all. She wasn't exactly sure how to go about shopping for someone, but she went into town anyhow and happened to see a girl she knew he would like in a bakery window. She went in and made a financial proposition. The girl said, 'Let's talk it over,' and they went next door and had a cup of coffee.

"At breakfast Ledlie found a note under his plate explaining his present. He was quite pleased with Celia, and she with herself. She wished him a happy day, kissed him goodbye, and went swimming at a pond in Wellfleet, and then had dinner with some friends—the present was to arrive at noon and she had left two bottles of champagne on ice—and when she got home after dark, Ledlie was sitting by the fire, all in one piece, but rather uncommunicative and sleepy.

"There was an uncorked bottle of champagne on the kitchen counter with about two glasses gone. The other was empty in the middle of the unmade bed. One of her veils must have been lifted, though perhaps not all the way. She picked up his cane—I forgot to mention he limped—and smashed her acquariums one by one, going around the room while he sat with his well-bred and amiable impassivity as if nothing in particular were taking place, but they both got their feet wet and that was the end of her interest in fish."

She looked out the window with narrowed eyes.

"So?" I said.

"I've got to go," she said. "Celia wasn't much of a painter then, but she was arrogant."

"What an unaccountable story!" I said. "Well, it won't be the first I ever got from you. Remember 'The Exile's Revenge'?"

"Yes. In which you ruined a perfectly good idea of mine."

"I was trying for a higher truth," I said icily.

"You ruined it completely. You didn't understand it."

She got up, pulling her coat around her, and I followed her out. My heart shrank at the blank day ahead.

"Where are you off to?" I said, but she only waved and shuffled toward town. A late fall snow was pelting down in clumps like islands that obliterated my glasses.

She had gone half a block before I got them off. She turned, straightened her back, lifted her chin and called, "Courage!" rolling her *r*s resoundingly. "Courage!"

Scenes

Back when I first came to town I used to drink on the beach with a whole lot of guys you know, some living, some dead. Women too. It was great fun, it really was. We had a great time from about ten o'clock in the morning till dark—or you passed out, or went to work or whatever, and if anybody got bored they could always go in the Fo'c'sle or the O.C. and have a few indoors.

And sooner or later somebody'd show up with a fish or some clams, and then we'd all head for whoever's house and have a feed. It was all very sedate. Antic but sedate. You know what I mean.

Every once in a while the cops would come and cart away the dump furniture we'd accumulated so we didn't have to sit in the sand. It was like our living room. We got loud sometimes but nobody complained.

In New York in those days there was a term for things like that. It would have been called a scene.

That was back before the drugs came in. I couldn't believe it, it all happened so fast. I remember I was sitting in the sand one day with some people leaning back against a driftwood log. We were drinking beer, and I looked over beside me, and this guy had a needle in his arm.

There was a corollary saying in New York—*Scenes do not last.* I always wanted to put that line in a poem, but I could never work it in. Maybe you can. *Scenes do not last.*

The Best Thing

You never had hot dog stew? Real Portagee hot dog stew? Oh no, it's the greatest. Oh yeah! I haven't made one of them in a long time. I'll tell you how you do it, you can go home and make one for yourself tonight.

You get some Black Angus hot dogs. If you can't, Oscar Mayers all right. Then you get a frying pan, you grease it all up. Then you chop up the hot dogs and some onions, and you sauté them up till they're nice and crisp.

Meanwhile that's going on you take another sauce pan and you put the tomatoes in—canned tomatoes, stew tomatoes, you know the kind I mean—and that's when you add your salt and pepper, your garlic, hot peppers, oregano and like that.

When that gets bubbling good you throw the dogs and the onions in, you stir them all around, and then you let it simmer a good long while, till all the tastes get brewed nice and smooth. You'll see.

Then—here's the trick—you put it in the refrigerator. You don't touch it that first day. You don't even go near it. It's always better the second day. Never eat it that first day. Don't even taste it. Of course you got to have will power. And something else in the house to eat.

But that second day, Pard, you won't even believe me how delicious it'll be. It's even better the third day. So—long as you're at it you might as well make a lot.

Homage to the Flip Flop

I put them on as soon—keep them on as long—as weather permits. April Fool's to Thanksgiving, with luck.

Uncle Sam gave me that inalienable joy: freedom from shoes.

My first pair came gratis at Lackland Air Force Base—only they were called shower shoes. I never saw them used.

I first tried mine about 1967, when bars and restaurants banned bare feet. The rationale was the owners didn't want you to get cut on a piece of glass and sue them, or that feet were more unsanitary or unsightly than footwear, but it was really the start of the end of the old P-town.

Once sold everywhere for pennies, they are fast disappearing. The future is faux sandals from $12.95 to the sky, like ribbon and crepe paper tire treads that won't last till July Fourth, much less Labor Day.

The real things are not faddish, and last at least a month, unless you're loss prone. And your feet are always grimy, and so are your sheets, and maybe your mate won't think they're so great, especially when winter comes and your calluses molder and slough off in crumbles and slabs. And they take getting used to. Every spring for the first few years the thong cleaves the tender flesh between your toes. Eventually your feet get so tough you can dance barefoot on a shell driveway. Toes grow independent and prehensile. I could never get rid of my athelete's foot till I started wearing flip-flops, but as soon as I put shoes on again it came right back.

Caveats: They're unstable. Climbing is out. They're a hindrance on the beach, imposssible in the dunes, though they're nothing to carry between two fingers. One stubbed toe is like another, each sworn to be the last. Don't jump from high places; flip-flops won't fit a cast. Never miss a chance to walk in wet grass says Joe Bones. Flee big guys in out-of-town bars with heavy boots who belly up close and say, "If I wore shit-kicks like those I'd be afraid someone would stomp on them." As for nails, glass, diamonds, watch where you're going. A light foot is never amiss. And rain on paved surface is treacherous, till instinct masters antitheses. Not only are the bald soles slippery on the street, but wet feet slide on the slick insole. A wrong reflex can accelerate a double skid, pull a groin muscle when a foot zips out and arms shoot up like a gingerbread man catching a trapeze. A rakish eyebrow may be raised briefly by one aloft on Commercial Street amid the amazed, shod mob.

By fall you can walk ten miles barefoot if you have to and feel no burn till dawn. There's a thrill in that, a deep satisfaction. You're still an animal, after all.

As far as flip-flops go, once you've learned to run in them you've arrived, though by then, of course, you don't need them.

Constant Concupiscence

She got more hurtful every year. And every year I minded more. Though I didn't know her name somehow I learned her husband's license plate while I slept with Sybil the poet.

But we always nodded hello on the street. Her eye was civil, grave and discreet. As time went by she seemed to be single. Her lips got rosier, her ass more round, her long blond hair streamed on the wind as she sailed the town on her bicycle, and I strolled with Belinda the painter.

Blind life, dark world kept turning. Soon she was selling me the morning paper, catching my coin dropped warm in her palm from fingers that never touched hers; but propinquity, blocked by the counter, proved prickly, routine, dismissive on her side, despondent on mine, for what's left after *Thanks* but *You're welcome?*

Then home to share the inexorably grisly world news at breakfast with Camilla the potter.

Thus I felt more reprieved than deprived the day in her stead a grizzled man stood, fierce eyed and full of indignant scorn for the rotten oligarchs in Washington. I would have lingered, lent ear, joined in his headline furors and derision of cant, nor left before we'd sated ourselves with the common solace of praise for the weather, whatever it was, enjoyed the uncompromising comradery of the defrauded but undeceived, had I not been so mad to recover the pure corporeality of Mona the sculptor.

Epochs came and epochs went. She of the piquant tits, classical hips and rich lips had jobs, I had lovers. She became a waitress—roving, ubiquitous—and wherever I took my latest love she was always there to attend, till I wished I'd stayed home alone.

Next she ruined the bar, my last resort and refuge, a dim, sullen den of stolid, unkempt, oblivious men, where I plied my muse and blurred like a shadow to dream.

Now where earwig had bred and cricket skreaked an electric fireplace glowed. Fresh flowers, blithe jazz, big prices, chic booze cozied a sociable crowd and ousted the old—all but me, though by then I choked on felicities, always committed to someone new, in the end condemned to answer, *Another?* with, *No thanks, Good night* and *Sleep tight.*

While the place got ever-more fancy she was raising a mountain of bills nightly in the felt-bottomed church oblation plate, seldom abashed by the cheap chink of change, where the avid vied for her favor with fives.

For she was a great ring master, served all alike with easy grace, quick behind the bar, lithe among the tables. Regal-eyed, still as steel, she could cut a lecher's innuendo off or blight a bleary compliment with the least aversion of countenance.

Always dressed to knockum dead, she adapted shows of chameleon decorum, one slow night even playing the bawd, ferociously whorish for some muddled middle Americans, who aspired to slum, but had to flee by the end of Act I, wives before, wives abaft.

Nightly I swilled more than my fill, made doodles instead of the next day's notes, and got such a habit of enchantment amongst the busy Sybarites, that I stayed away in dismay one night and never went back, waited elsewhere for the late-reading scholar Yolanda.

Various came and went before I tried my old haunt again, drawn by pristine boredom to see if her spell could still bind, found all changed to nouveau antique decor—objets d'art, gilt mirrors, plush sofas—with a winsome gay queen presiding over a final gentility, where never would blunder a creature so crass as a female, so back I went to street wanderlust and my annual dilemma of how and with whom to weather the winter.

Meanwhile where had my paragon gone? For whom would she have abandoned her avocation for a mere vacation?

No love, no place, no sense to life, but books and the daily dying. Man in mad want pursues meaning, but gets no rest without a mate.

The Muslim, allowed four wives, yet thinks the chador wise, knowing those enigmatic, glowing eyes prove all religion lies.

In the profane West men still contend for power, riches, sheer joy of strife, but the modern rounder takes sword to no Troys, but mouselike explores boondocks or bars.

Well, with the help of Rhoda the lithographer I forgot her till the next unsettling sign of the times spelled an end to Ye Olde Shoppe, quaint & cunnin, where since 1915 the DeSouza DaSilva clan had sold souvenirs and gewgaws to blue-collar families that worked the other fifty weeks a year.

Pink-nippled mermaids, buoys and gulls, bayberry-scented sachets, scrimshaw, samplers embroidered Cape Cod, Mass, lacquered plaques depicting slightly risqué jokes with fat-bottomed wives as the butt, rose-tinted prints of the Kennedys, haloed popes, pudgy cupids, plaster turds, rubber squid, pyramids of abalone shells from Key West, paraffin-sealed jars of beach plum jelly—all had vanished, the place renamed Baubles, Bibelots, Bagatelles: a boutique.

I went in to buy my love some trifle to mark the summer solstice, start the longest, most languid season, sublime with instant nostalgia of certain decline, found my nemesis ensconced amidst finery fit to trick out a global seraglio—saucy camisoles, saris, sarongs, harem veils, bustiers, kimonos, peignoirs, excruciating lingerie and a brutal mix of incense and musk, which made it hard to leave, unnerving to stay, the shop empty, the door shut, long, meek steps to retreat to the street where boatloads of daytrippers traipsed.

She acted eerily (we had never in truth been introduced) as if I were the Tourist Compleat and she no washashore. *Your lady's pleasure?* her madam's voice purred.

My conflated memories clashed, and resorting to fustian I declared for a touch of cachet and a taste of panache.

God knows what I boded by mots like those but what I got was the business. Pitiless Pandora unbarred her boudoir, mock-modeled her intimate wares in turn, all with a shimmy of hips, bouncing tits and impudent eye, while I throbbed in my throes at the many in one and vice versa—and finally chose the orange boa that seemed most to entrance her. Behind the counter, demure once again, she gave me an unconscionable discount, still ten times what I intended to spend.

I should have left it looping the first pole I passed, to ensnare some hesitant babe and her horny swain, but took it home to wrong Rhoda, for whom, ecstatic, it overnight became such a fetish that henceforth she wouldn't be bedded without it, which caused me a certain doleful disquiet, till the condo plague and greed-crazed rents drove her and the last of the transients from town and I met her successor, the rich etcher Francesca, access to whose treasure, lacking an exact je ne sais quoi, merely jaded me more.

How I wish I had better than doggerel for the long-dreamt-of night inevitable fate made us endure as equals, inebriates both on the right side of Moon's bar, elbow to elbow, thigh to thigh, in November, that blustery, sweet sequel to limp Labor Day, when shops close down, and cash is no longer the one game in town.

Recuperational, flush, awash in communal concord, the inveterate denizens daily got off on smooching adieux while delaying departure for The Islands, Key West, Lisbon, Capri, or hibernation, TV and a favorite couch, their auras aglow with the aphrodisia of leisure.

Her hornet-blue eyes paralyzed mine. Her lips blurred, her bodice was coming undone when she slurred, *Let's switch to champagne, we'll party, I'll pay,* then laid her hand in my lap and rode her stool like a leaping dolphin.

I can't, I replied, resolutely dismounted, and her derisive laughter hied me home hard, baffled and dumb to Rosa the composer.

Fidelity stingy, pedantic, absurd! I should have had her and she me, maybe. But how foretell if the morrow will bring lucid resolve or distraction? For want indulged becomes need the next night, a taste an insatiable craving. Perhaps petty lusts are best untested, real passions fled, the urge to digress curbed, the ever-virgin world of novel amours well left at the desk to the never-chastened imagination.

Regrets are egregious, retrospects vain, life is merely mad strivings. Even is what I meant to get for the times she had tormented me, partly was hoping to spare and be spared, tame greed to the patience of timing, till we both could licitly lie down in some uncomplicated Elysium, but the dismal deferral of old desire proved only the morbidity of morality, for one clear line between the sexes is a woman may say *No*, and *No*, and *No* again, but a man wrongs unless he says *Yes*. She has a choice but he has none.

Lawless female beauty lives to risk its will, and male must yield to female, though their only bond be sensual, lest denial fix a jinx in both. Thus women squander their pride, and men betray them.

After that I passed her shop daily, too sheepish to glance in. She averted her eyes on the street and shunned my dreams, while another year whirled by or maybe two or three—Diana, Susanna, Priscilla, Drusilla—I mix them up, I can't keep track. It was always too soon to look back.

Then came one of those balmy spring days that take you by surprise. I saw her grubbing in a planter as I happened along, felt a pulse of pleasure start, rejoiced that we had paid our exile out, were now restored to happier realms.

But then I noticed her new assistant. The closer I got the more beleaguered I grew, for she, barely past girlhood, dazzled like dew at bright dawn after a foggy, bat-torn night, and was immortally formed.

I stared from her to my old idol, whose back hurt from bending and who, hands in the dirt, gave me a steadily fading gaze of welcome as she saw me losing control of my eyes, and at the last moment, as I passed by struck dumb, bowed again to her pansies, while the guileless one smiled.

I kept on home and took to my desk, a raft of dismay in a sea of guilt. I couldn't go back and say, *Pardon me, but that's just the injustice of the power of youth. Given a real choice I'd surely choose you for all the long-held furies, for the sorrows and rights of the unlived life,* nor could I even have sworn it was true.

After that I couldn't have caught her eye had I gone gay or jumped off the Pilgrim Monument.

There my tale might have ended, but for the rule of coincidence upon a possible world. I found her discarded books in a thrift shop, inscribed with her maiden name. She had kept nothing apparently, not even her Norton Anthologies. There they were: Raleigh, Blake, Coleridge, Keats, et al., nakedly disposed amid the trash—*Astrology for You* and *Diet for Two, Nanny Goat Goes to Rome, The Message is Massage* and *How to Tame a Ménage*—the whole mauled library of her teaching days before domestic life claimed her, and now the need for shelf space. Or was it a final, despairing surrender? I bought them all.

Much I munched on her marginalia, mulling our common ways, and unaware parting.

Whereat she single-mindedly got so rich, vending androgynous international chic, that she hired yet another darling clerk, and kept out of the shop, acquiring a fantastic tan, while I got bedsores on my ass from desk life, and fought off my yen to glance in.

Time slips by inconstantly. We miss the moment turning, everything changing. One summer she spent on her threshold, blank eyed, impersonally smiling like any bourgeois, grew fat, hennaed her hair, wore makeup masks, the jewelry and robes of a dissolute dowager. Did she notice how bald, how bent I'd got?

She an owner, slave of increase, I a doubter, dumb with decay, the dewey one got married, left town, and the other darling too grew into womanhood and went, while I pursued the sweet vagrant Maria.

What secret catastrophes daily strike, faces melting on the street, for their love has left them on their birthday for their best friend, or a screw is turned till a silent scream begins.

More to read than write, the time to live is always now, but not forever can eros rule hypothetical sorrows grown real. Heart flags, not to mention liver, brain cells, lungs. And the pen must find other inspiration.

The Fo'c'sle, Piggy's, the old A-House, all are gone into other things. Commercial Street is a shopping mall, longevity the main social scene.

I seldom see her anymore. She moved to Boston. Her shop sells real estate. She came down on weekends for a while, then seldom.

One year she was thin again, the next enormous, last, surpassing any past radiance, pushing a baby carriage, her happy husband beside her.

But when I mull life's mysteries and remember dreams untold, how I wearied of others, but never of her, too fond of women or not fond enough, to give us both due credit, I still get so hard it hurts.

Ashes

I don't know what's going on. But something's happening. Something . . . sneaky. I know that much. Maybe I've reached a certain age. I don't mean the hot flashes. Them I can stand. They come and they go. I'm prepared for that. No. It's something out there, not in me. Whatever it is though I know one thing—I can't take it anymore. Let me out of here!

First it was my mother. I shouldn't complain. She had an easy death. She didn't even know what death was. She had Alzheimer's. I couldn't even stand to go see her. At the funeral? In the coffin? I just took one quick peep. She was like a wax doll with a permanent wave and all this rouge. It was really eerie. Like a dream? I can't stand things like that. Her mouth was twisted in a way it never was in real life. Or maybe I never noticed it before. I feel bad I never went to see her after those first few times. She almost didn't know me, even then. What can you do? Go on a toot, I guess. I went on plenty of toots these last few years.

I'll probably have to go on another one next week, just to get through. Anton's giving Bonnie a combination fiftieth birthday and thirtieth wedding anniversary party. Big family pow-wow in that palace of chandeliers and balconies he built her. It's going to be horrible. I can't bear to see her, but I can't not go. She's dying of a little tiny lesion from a couple of years ago, and now it's spread all through her. She keeps asking questions no one can answer. She can't really grasp that she's dying. Neither can Anton. He just bought her another horse.

It makes me sick to think. She's one of the most easy-going women I know, one of the most beautiful too. From the neck down you'd never think she had three kids. Her face is like a road map of all the great places she's been. Really enviable lines. I wouldn't mind looking like her. They had a happy marriage. He never ran around on her.

I haven't been to see her since the word got out. I made her a medicine wheel—like a dream catcher? I designed it to hold her long braid that was cut off before they started chemo. I haven't been able to get up the nerve to give it to her, mainly because I can't figure out how to get the braid.

My dream catcher is a real beauty though. It has a hole to let the bad dreams out and another for the good ones to get in. It's got rawhide fringes and shells and bluejay feathers and sterling silver fish—birds in flight, fish free in the sea.

I'll go to this party if I have to. I'll give it to her then, if I dare. I still don't know how to get that braid. I'd like to wrap myself up in it for a while. Well, I'll do what I do. It all depends on what happens.

Anyway this is not so bad as Janet because with her we both knew but neither of us was sure if the other knew and anyway neither of us would admit it was true, even if it was true. I still don't know how I got through that one.

She never had any luck. She let herself be captivated by a whole string of vile boyfriends. The last one was a junkie. He lost his job, she was supporting him, working two jobs. When she got sick he split. She said he felt terrible, but he was too sensitive, he couldn't bear to see her like that. Not bringing in any money, I guess he meant.

She had a brain tumor, but they couldn't figure it out at first, why her foot wouldn't work. She didn't think she was going to die. Nobody would tell her, including the doctors. They just said it wasn't a good idea to operate. By then it was too late, I guess. She never would have let them cut on her anyway. She doesn't believe in that sort of thing—invasive medicine, toxic drugs, all that Western stuff. Finally they just sent her home.

That really cheered her up, convinced her she was going to get better. Me too. I couldn't believe she was going to die. She had all these remedies she got from the reservation. She lived with an Indian family for a while, but there was too much drunken violence and antiwhite . . . whatever. And the guy beat her up. But she learned a lot about nature. That's how we got to be friends, we would both go to the powwows up in Mashpee.

Finally she got so bad she needed a wheelchair. So they took up a collection, put a coffee can on the bar at the Old Colony. After a few days there was quite a wad in there. Some guy, not one of the regulars, he was probably just joking—he said, "In this place the money's bound to get filched."

Everybody got all indignant. They gave him so much shit he went next door to drink. And wouldn't you know! The money got filched.

I made her a dream catcher too—but I never dared to give it to her. I don't think she would have appreciated it, she wasn't ready yet for the happy hunting ground. Actually it was the best one I ever made. It had all these Jamaican gris-gris beads and charms, and right in the middle a cough ball from an owl. I don't know why I put that in there, I guess I thought she would like it. Of course she never saw it. I did bring it to the funeral though.

Charlotte adored it. She kept asking in this hoarse whisper if she could have it. She was starting chemo herself in a couple of days. I kept saying, "Whatever, whatever, if it works out." It felt a little weird because I'd made it specially for Janet.

It was December, freezing cold. It started at three o'clock on the beach at Herring Cove and was supposed to last till the sun went down. I hate funerals. Kimball and I went to the Vet's and had a few before we even got there.

Tarkin had his truck in the parking lot with a boom box on the hood playing Janet's collection of Indian chants. And a big jug of Bloody Marys and some chips and salsa. We never could get a fire going. The cab of the truck was the only place you could get warm. There was only room for one of us at a time because the dogs were all in there. They all sat in the front seat looking out the windshield at the ocean just like people, they didn't want to go outside either.

Kimball and I brought a bottle of Eileen's favorite Cuervo tequila. Obie's wife brought white wine as usual. McKenzie had been on the wagon for sixteen days but he had to get off for this. Dit'n Dat were there. They don't really look anything alike, but they've always got the same expression on their face. One of them —I forget which—says he reads quantum physics just to keep his mind off AIDS. Herbert was there with his camera, recording everything for posterity. God knows who'll be around to watch it. And a couple of Lesbians. I think Janet might have been in that scene for a little while, got fed up with men maybe. Even Ruby D was there. They hadn't spoken for years, they used to be good friends. I can't remember now what that was about, they probably didn't either. There was a woman from the hospice. I guess she goes to a lot of funerals, I don't know how she does it. Orin was there with his enormous pecs in just a sweatshirt, he says, "I'm not cold." U-turn Sue from Montreal was there. Cupcake and Princess were there. And Mudbone and Muffy. And Abby and Fred, he was taking the opportunity to get a snootful, she doesn't even let him out of the house anymore. He admits he's pussy whipped, he's happy I guess. When he goes to have a haircut, the minute he gets out the door, she calls the barber with instructions. All she has to say is, "Furr-rredd-duhh," and he comes trotting. She tried it just once that day. He didn't pay any attention, he was off his leash out there. So I guess she just said the hell with it, and had a few herself. A lot of other people were there. I forget. A lot of the old gang is gone too, there in spirit, I guess.

We finally gathered on the beach and sang her favorite song, "Suzanne takes you down." Then Kay gave a short prayer, just a standard Christian riff. Nobody really knew what to do. We had the ashes in an urn—we were going to save half of them to scatter in the dunes next summer. Kimball all of a sudden grabbed the urn and toddled down to the water, took the top off and just whirled around like a dervish baby. You could see the ashes sail off on the wind, like a lot of Mayflies. Then he threw the urn in and yelled, "Bon Voyage!"

Sometimes his whimsy gets you know a bit crass. People didn't know whether to laugh or what. Then he grabbed my dream catcher and heaved *it* in. I didn't really want Charlotte to have it anyway. It was quite majestic. The tide was going out. You could see it bobbing out there for a long time.

Of course Charlotte was disappointed. But I made her another one. She had short hair to start with. I think what I got was pubic hair anyway. In a little locket? Her boyfriend gave it to me. Actually he was more upset than she was. She couldn't afford to get too bent. She was the one who smoked all the cigarettes, not that he doesn't smoke like a fiend himself. Anyway, it must have been a good one, maybe it worked, because she got better.

After everything went in the drink there wasn't much left to do. Everyone huddled around the truck and then people drifted away except for the hard core like yours truly who wouldn't dream of leaving till the sun went down. I was frozen stiff. Actually, it was a fantastic sunset—sort of orange and purple and then a little green halo at the end. So all in all it wasn't a bad funeral. It was just right somehow. Macabre is what it was. Janet would've loved it.

I'm driving Kimball back. He says, "Everybody's going to the O.C." I'm saying to myself, "Why am I doing this? I don't want another drink," but then I thought, "What choice do I have? I can't just go home at this hour." I wound up staying till midnight. Even with all I drank I never got a buzz on.

There's been a lot of change. I guess that's what it is. Nothing's the same. All the things that started out so copacetic all went kaflooey. Everybody's alone now. Half the town's gay.

I haven't been with anybody since Willie? Five years ago? What a battle we had! Lasted about ten years. He wanted me to stay home, be his obedient little housefrau. While he was out every night catting around. He had a temper, he was completely reckless, he didn't care what happened to him. I think it came from seeing his friends get killed in Vietnam. When he got drinking and talking about it, he'd get wild, it was like he was talking in tongues, and then watch out! He'd pick on strangers three times his size. I kept leaving him. He didn't care, so I always went back. I loved his hair. He had beautiful long hair. It's not like we were always fighting each other. One time the cops were trying to arrest him. They were having a hard time getting him cuffed, there were five of them and they couldn't handle him. I ran out of the O.C. just when this one cop raised his billy club. I grabbed his arm, his nose got smashed on the upswing when he broke my grip. The cops and the judge like Willie. He's eloquent in court, he's had a lot of practice. I got all the blame, cost me a lot of money.

I did have one little something-or-other. Right after Willie. With Jinson? He's what the local girls call cunnin. He's all brag and swagger. He's always well dressed, he's vibrant, but when I'm tempted I feel that little gouge on my cheek from his ring where he hit me that one time. I never let him near me again. He came up to me one night, not so long ago either. I was sitting here, just an innocent barstander as usual. He begins to wind his finger in my hair. He says, "There's something romantic about those earrings I gave you."

I says, "Yeah. Kinda. Sorta." I wince to think of the pretty young things he finds to fuck him.

I should have sicced him on this babe who showed up in town last summer. She was trying to make a splash. She wasn't bad looking, but nobody would have anything to do with her. If she'd just sat there like a good little girl all the scavengers would have been all over her like flies on dead bait. You've got to be a little bit aloof.

Just so she wouldn't feel like the only one who ever got rejected, I said I hadn't got laid in umpteen years, there were no men here worth having anymore, blah-blah-blah.

Next thing I know she's nuzzling up to me, asking about my living arrangements, did I have an extra bed? I began to get pretty cagey. I wouldn't even tell her my address.

Finally she made friends with Duncan. You know what a nice guy he is, he couldn't say no to a vampire. So she spent two nights on his couch. Meanwhile she's sniffing around the bars trying to find a live one. He's a gentleman, he never molested her.

She's telling me all this. I know Duncan's lonely. I can't remember the last time he had anybody. So I said, just to be funny, just to be helpful actually, I said, "You're there, you might as well enjoy yourself. He's great in bed."

"Oh, really?" she says.

"Oh, yes," I says. "He's very well endowed."

She says, "Really?"

I said, "I mean I've heard."

So next thing I know she's sleeping with Duncan. He's going around with this crooked grin on his face, he can't help himself. And then one morning he wakes up and she's gone, and his wallet, and his watch, also his car keys, not to mention his car. So he goes back to bed, he figures she's gone to the store.

After a couple of days he had to tell the cops. Duncan refuses to believe anything bad about her, he's got this idea that she had some family emergency and she's going to bring the car back some day.

She's just some greenhorn hustler who'll probably show up next summer expecting nobody to remember her.

Well, that's the bar life, the kind of things you have to hear, some funny, some not so funny. The other day I was sitting here minding my own business, trying to get a buzz on. It's not so easy as you might think. You can put a big hole in a paycheck and get nothing but a depression.

Anyway, Paula and Dolores came in. I couldn't help but hear every word. Not that I'd try not to. What's the use? Things go on whether you know about them or not.

Paula's in tears, she must be fifty-five, sixty. Apparently she was on bad terms with her ninety-one-year-old mother. She's saying to Dolores, in this little girl's voice, "I do my best, Ma. I'm not smart like Jimmy, but I do my best."

"Oh, brothers!" Dolores says. "I know all about brothers!"

Paula says, "Nothing I do is ever right. She always complains. I could never satisfy her. I went over there every single day of my life after Dad died. Jimmy shows up at Christmas and maybe Thanksgiving. He always sits in Dad's chair, she brings him beers. She idolizes him. He never does a dish. I'm supposed to be a servant that doesn't even get thanked. Why is she always so mean to me? Finally I just walked out. After all these years. I don't think I'm ever going to see her again. I think I'm cracking up."

Dolores says, "Do you love her?"

Paula says, "Of course I do, she's my ma. I always loved her, but she never loved me. Jimmy was the one she loved."

Dolores said, "Have you ever told her you love her?"

Paula thinks a long time, then she shakes her head.

Dolores says, "You call her up right now and tell her you love her. Before it's too late."

Paula says, "I can't."

Dolores says, "You can. You can. You call her up right now. You hear me? Before it's too late. Here's a dime."

The phone's right behind them. Paula sat there shaking her head and crying, she wasn't even drinking her drink. I was looking the other way, as much as I could. Too bad your ears won't turn. Dolores got really fervent. She said, "You tell her you love her before it's too late."

Paula just sat there shaking her head, I could see the tears flying.

Dolores said—she almost got in tears herself—she said, "The same thing happened to me. I had a fight with my daughter. We never made it up. We had lots of fights. I was in the right every time, as it happens. That's what made it so hard. I wanted to tell her I loved her but I never did. It doesn't matter now how right I was. She died and we were never reconciled. I never got to hold her in my arms and tell her I loved her."

Paula kept nodding. She kept promising she'd call her mother right up, but all I saw was they ordered another round. By that time they were like two Niagara Falls. These weeping women! I had to get the hell out of there. In my family my sister was the good one, I was the bad one, but my mother never chose. She always treated us the same. At least I don't have a daughter to worry about. Or despise me. Or abandon me.

I went home and worked in my garden. That's always a relief, that's my only respite now. I was getting compost, I tunneled down to the bottom. It was almost solid worms. There were more worms than compost. I wonder what that means. Well, my roses are doing great. I can't believe it's 1990 already. And this is still Provincetown, though it doesn't always feel like it.

Mervyn Boddicky's brother just went by. I should go see him. I hate to. He looks awful. He's beginning to show it, he's just getting to the point where I began to believe that Mervyn was really sick, that maybe it really was going to happen to him. That was when I began to go see him every day, take him soup and wash his clothes, look after his hair. He went downhill fast after that.

His brother's gay too. Both of his brothers. And his sister too. I miss him so much. He was so handsome when I first knew him. He was everybody's heartthrob. I didn't know he was gay. We flew down to Haiti together. I had my hopes up. Achille met us at the airport in Port-au-Prince with a cab. We stopped off at his favorite place. It was upstairs in this big open bar, you could look down and see people milling. Haiti takes getting used to. There were some prostitutes parading around. I didn't know what they were at first. Being as we were Blans, they swarmed out of the woodwork, and right away Achille went off with one of them.

The whorehouse was right next door. He came back with a guy and Mervyn went off with him. There were men there too. That's how I found out he was gay. Boy was I shocked! And disappointed! I drank the cab driver literally under the table and we had to take a tap-tap to the hotel.

But we got to be good friends. I really miss him. I could use some new gay friends. I was never really close with his brother. Now I don't want to make friends with him. Isn't that awful? You don't want to get to know someone because you know they're going to die.

Mervyn never even had a funeral. He absolutely forbade it. So nothing happened. He died and that was all. But there's something strange about it. It's like we're still waiting, it's like he's still around. I keep thinking I see him, but then it turns out to be his brother. It's like I'm going to have to go through it all over again. Maybe his brother'll have a funeral at least. I might like to go to that one. I might feel better. Maybe. At funerals you get to let it all out. Sometimes.

Not like Teresa's though. Well, she had two. The first one was on the beach, very conventional, lots to eat and drink. People went for a swim. Very decorous. Except for her sons. They got into a fight and had to be separated. One of them idolized her, he's very clean-cut, married, living out West. The other one's a bum and hates everybody in town because he thinks everybody hates him because he's her son. The one that loved her said she was the best mother anyone ever had. The other calls her a scumbag. She wrote her own obituary. Of course it was all lies. She gave the *Clarion* a picture of herself when she was young. Very beautiful, very glamorous when she first came here. You'd never connect that picture with the face she ended up with.

She was a volatile character when she was having her children and hanging out in the O.C., very hospitable too. She always had a houseful of people. Then all of a sudden like fifteen years ago she reformed. She was all good works. She got a responsible job, she began looking after her kids, she never drank another drop, she quit smoking. She got very respectable. Self-righteous. Sanctimonious. She harassed everybody about recycling. She became a vegetarian. She'd spot you in a restaurant, she was like the food police. She was like one of those women who'd eat their own placenta. And she did a lot of good for the poor too. She took on the powers that be, she was on all these committees. She was a real fighter. Also crazy as a loon. I guess that's what happens when the reformed become reformers.

A lot of people didn't go to her funeral. I thought it was strange. But people are busy or they don't find out or whatever. And it was summer.

But she'd made some really serious enemies of her old friends. She'd reverted to her old self. They didn't mind her when she was horrible before, but I guess they didn't like it when she took up her old ways again.

It started when she thought she had cancer a couple of years before she actually died. She was very bitter, very vengeful, like she expected to live forever now that she was a good person. She said she was going to take certain people with her. She sounded like she meant it. She even named names—not mine fortunately. She scared some people. She was always into occult stuff. They didn't know what she might do.

So they sort of banded together and had their own little séances like witchcraft where they tried to put a hex on her, telepathize her cancer to kill her quick.

Then it turned out she didn't have cancer after all. And then she got even more menacing. All her old friends were devastated. They'd been counting on her to kick off. She was very happy to disappoint them. By that time, nobody was forgiving anybody, nobody was making peace. You'd think with a new lease on life she might have considered going back to her better self, but oh, no, she got just worse and worse, like she was making up for lost time. And she was still adding to her doom and death list. She told everybody who she was performing her Satanic rituals on. She spread it around that they'd all be dead in a year. She was going to fill up the graveyard. And the proof of it was that she'd cured her cancer by giving it to them.

It was pretty hairy, whether you believe in that stuff or not. She was at a party at Kay's and she toasted their coming deaths. She says, "Here's cancer to this one, here's a thrombosis to that one, here's meningitis to this other one." And you could just see them keeling over, she fit the disease to the type all right.

That was too much, even for Kay, who finally asked her to leave. On her way out she took two bottles of booze. And nobody dared to say anything. Kay's very airy, she's like a Buddha—she didn't even get angry. She said, "Teresa always does things like that." Of course Teresa hadn't done any of that stuff in years.

So I'm sitting in the O.C. Day after the funeral? Duncan comes in, he says, "You going to the red funeral?"

I says, "The red funeral?"

He says, "Yeah. Right out back."

I had no idea what he meant. I finished my drink, I went out.

Ashes

All her enemies are sitting up against a big log in the sand. They've got a cooler full of champagne and a whole box of plastic champagne glasses and a tape deck with curses and spells they'd made, and they've all got something red on. Kimball had a red tie, I've never seen him in a tie before. Kay was there too, she was the only one with nothing red on. They were toasting Teresa in hell. They says, "The harpie is dead! Have a drink!" They were really savage, they were absolutely overjoyed.

I went right back in the O.C. That really scared me. I always think of funerals as being like a benediction. No matter who you are. No matter what you've done. I didn't want to be any part of this one. Not everybody gets two funerals though.

Nothing's the same anymore. Everybody's dried out, for one thing, or aged out, or left town. Or just . . . I don't know what. Like when Greg and Bill disappeared. How could that have happened? They were both experienced, they worked around boats all their lives. The last time anyone saw them it was a beautiful day, they had a half-gallon of Jim Beam and they were just out rowing around. Nobody saw them for a week, nobody worried. They might have been anywhere, gone to Mexico, gone to The Islands, god knows. They were buddies. Then their boat washed up on Long Point. And then there started to be rumors about foul play. Everybody had a theory, people looking at each other, making bets. Which one did in the other one and went where?

And then they were both found on the breakwater. Only about ten yards apart. Somehow they just got out of the boat and drowned. Both of them. I mean they were real water people, seamen. They used to fish. Back when there were fish.

Even the boats are falling apart. Three wrecks on the beach at the same time and the owners can't afford to have them towed away. They're worthless. People sleeping in them. I guess there were always people living on the beach. Only the winters are worse now. Even the weather's fucked up.

There's only a handful of real fishermen left in town. I wonder what I'm doing here myself. Once in a while. Boats from New Bedford come in. These beautiful guys with their good-humored faces. They have this great laughter, way down in the chest. They all have wives at home. Naturally. And they're faithful, they're good Catholics. They stick together, they only have a few. They don't get rambunctious. They don't even speak English. Well, that's a relief sometimes.

I remember Marla coming in one day—you know how tall she is—she says, "I'm fed up with being taken for a TV every time I put my good clothes on."

Maybe I should have left right then. You get used to things. It's like you've grown cataracts, you stop seeing what's right in front of you. Whichever road you choose though there always comes a certain time of disappointment when you look back and see all the other roads just winding out of sight.

How we got to this point I do not know. It's like everything went from hunky-dory to shipping water overnight. Everybody's getting evicted. They're going to condo my whole building. I've got a year to get out, but Kirby Flynn is just about out on the street already. He hasn't paid any rent in five months.

He lives upstairs from me. He's very handsome, charming, witty. He's half in, half out of the closet. Very macho. Hangs out in the straight bars, sits in the corner at the O.C. smoking menthols, one every half hour.

His dog Karma developed a tumor on its belly. I kept insisting he take it to the vet. I should have done it myself, but it's expensive. I should have done it anyway. More tumors came and more and more. It was terrible. Poor Karma! He could hardly drag himself around.

One night Kirby had Del Marr over. Del's this pathetic derelict who'll do anything for money. They got drunk and did whatever. Next morning Del was gone, and so was all of Kirby's money. His back rent was due that day. Or else! Out! I don't know where he got it, he wasn't working.

Anyway, when he went to look for Del he found Karma dead in his own mess on the landing. Del must have just stepped right over him on the way out. Kirby came and asked me to help him bury Karma, which I did. I didn't say a word. Kirby was in terrible shape, I guess he and Del drank all night. He was desperate because the landlord was coming at noon, so I made the rounds, I put the word out, and finally Del's brother showed up and said, "Don't worry, I'll take care of it." And he did too, in about one hour flat.

So, a couple of days later Kirby's sitting in the O.C. with Kay and a third person who shall remain nameless—needless to say no friend of either—because she couldn't wait to tell me that Kirby had said I wouldn't even loan him a pack of cigarettes when he was broke.

Kay says, "Ohhhh, that's the way she is sometimes. She can be an angel or she can be a bitch."

I confronted them both with it. Kay said she didn't remember any such conversation. She said my informant must have been projecting. Then she said Kirby never means anything he says anyway. That's Kay for you. Kirby just denied any of it ever happened.

That's Kirby too. He lies about his HIV. He says, "Oh, didn't I tell you?" He says he got it from a whorehouse down in Mexico. He insists on that one possibility, though he's been around this town forever. The only reason I even know is because one day he was sitting here all smiles. He's usually quite suave. I said, "What have you got to be so happy about?"

He said, "I'm celebrating. I just had my physical and I'm fine."

I said, "What's a physical cost these days?"

He says, "Er, I don't know."

I says, "Come on!"

He says, "Er."

I says, "You don't know?"

He says, "Errr. Five dollars."

"What?" I says. "Five dollars?"

He says, "I'm on a plan."

"What plan?" I says. "I'd like to get on that plan myself."

He says, "Errrr, didn't I tell you?"

He used to have Brad over. Somehow Brad's bimbo found out. Well, Kirby's perfectly capable of letting her know how things stood. She broke up with Brad immediately. She went and got an AIDS test that same day. And the next day she moved in with some guy in Chatham. She didn't even wait for the result. I wonder what she told *him*.

I took it up with Kirby. He said, "Oh, I only have safe sex."

"Safe sex?" I yelled at him. "What's that?"

Did he tell Brad? How far did his virus go? There he is, sitting at the end of the bar, smoking his cigarettes like clockwork. He looks healthy.

I mean what's going on? Is this the way people were brought up? The bar scene sure isn't what it used to be.

Last night on TV I got The Murder Channel by mistake. That's what I call it. They have these shows of animals killing each other, just the chase and the kill, predators and prey, just blood and guts. And now they've started to have storm shows, tornadoes, hurricanes, typhoons, weather disasters, pictures of wreckage. You'd think the news would be enough. Well, I don't watch that either.

I did see a good elephant program though—the herd was on this long trek to find water. The littlest one couldn't go on. It just lay down on the ground, and all the other elephants gathered around trying to help it up with their trunks. They stayed for six hours before they went on. They kept looking back, but they were desperate for water. The calf's mother stayed, just to comfort it, I guess, and then she stayed around for another whole day after it died. She'd start to go on and then she'd come back.

Elephants are so civilized! The two things I love most in the whole world—animals and weather—and it seems like they're both all screwed up too.

So now I'm looking at moving for the first time since I finally found a year-round place I could afford. I used to move twice a year, spring and fall. I don't know how I did it. I'm not as young as I was.

Actually I just realized it's not so much sneaky as spooky. It's like every corner you go around there's a mirror, only there's some stranger in it. I figure it all comes of having to decide what to throw out, what to keep.

My dogs, my cat, my birds, my plants, I was thinking of getting some fish. The paintings Achille bought in Haiti, they're mystical. The chair my Indian boyfriend made me. All my stupid good-luck charms, locks of hair in cellophane.

Boxes and boxes and boxes of what? Clothes? Mementos? I don't even know myself. How can I not know? And I'm scared to find out. What's to be scared of? It's only the past. And it's past. I think maybe if I look I'll regret everything. Like a day of reckoning.

Last week I came back from the A&P with about ten twenty pound bags of dog food, birdseed, cat litter. And there's Jackle in my winter parking place with his BMW. He just got back that minute from The Islands. He's got a sailboat, he's all tanned, he's got these gold chains around his neck. And he gives me the bird. You know, Up Yours!

I had to go park around the block. Then I had to make about ten trips up those steep stairs. It's a nice place, but it's old, the dirt's coming out of the walls, you can't keep it clean. Not to mention the fur. I'm not a great housekeeper.

So I'm standing there in my mess of a kitchen, I'm absolutely bullshit—wiping the sweat off my brow—and I happened to glance at my mantelpiece, and I see the urn with Greta's ashes. There's stuff piled up around it, so I don't have to see it all the time.

She was Jackle's girfriend in the old days, she wanted them strewn in the sea down in Jamaica. That was years ago, but he always said he'd do it. I kept reminding him. He'd say, "Yeah, yeah, next time I go."

And then he'd forget or I'd forget, and finally the whole thing got lost in the flow.

I stewed for a week about that arrogant bastard taking my parking place and laughing at me. He's one person that ought to be in jail. I got furious. He'd just opened his shop. I took the urn down. Right in the middle of the day. He had a big sale on. There were these two yuppies at the counter. He had all this gold spread out on the display case. I marched right up to them. He gave me this look with the eyebrows that said, *Later.*

"Oh, really?" I said, and plunked the urn down, lucky it didn't crack the glass. I said, "Here's that girlfriend you said you wanted."

Next day he says, "What are you, crazy? Right when I was making a sale!"

I said, "If you're going to give me the bird."

"What d'ya mean?" he says. "That was just a friendly greeting."

I said, "You know what the trouble with you is, Jack? You lack the social graces."

He'll probably just dump Greta and use the urn for an ashtray.

But it reminded me I've got these two other urns in my closet. They're even before Greta. They're not really mine. I inherited them from other people who died before they ever got around to disposing of them. One of them wanted to be scattered out at Hatches Harbor. It's beautiful out there. It's ghostly. The foghorn's always booming, even in the sun, if there's even the slightest touch of haze, and there always is, you know, that little chill on the skin? It's a long way. It's a nice walk. I kept meaning to do it. I don't even walk anymore. I don't swim. I don't do anything. It's just work and the O.C. now.

The other one, Rosy McCall, I forget where she wanted to go. Beech Forest, I think. I've got it written down somewhere. I only knew her through Achille. And he's dead too. Rosy McCall. She was a wild one, I heard, a real tough lady. Before my time though.

What happened is, I had a party—God, what a long time ago! That was the last party I ever gave—I put both those urns out of sight in the closet where I store junk I'll never have any use for, and there they still are. Unless they've got up and walked off. Like everything else.

How did things get like this? I guess I'll have to make some adjustments. Maybe I'll start with those urns. It gives me the creeps though even to think about them. Well, I'd rather be ashes in the wind than food for worms. Except then of course you've got to depend. I wonder who'll inherit mine.

Stop! Wait! Don't say a word. I'm having heart palpitations. Hold my hand, I think some guy just smiled at me. Must be straight, huh?! God, he looks like a real Gypsy! Doesn't he?

Noon, Afternoon, Night

You want to hear a story? I'll tell you a story about the story that's going around town about the two million dollar lottery ticket that got bought at Pilgrim Variety the other day.

You know how people try to keep things like that secret, they don't want anyone coming after them for a piece of the action. Everybody's still trying to figure out who it was.

What it was was Judy told Trudy who told Peggy she knew somebody who met somebody related to somebody's cousin who said she knew somebody whose boyfriend's sister overheard some dirt about whoever it was bought the ticket in some other town up Cape.

Last trip yesterday, the whales weren't cooperating, showed themselves infrequently and perfunctorily, and everybody was restive, bored, sunstroked, muttering about getting their money back.

The bridge thought they saw something, and the boat took a sharp turn. People ran to the bow to see what was up, and a woman pulled her hand out of her pocket too quick and a ten dollar bill flew out and blew away.

A bunch of people in the stern all started laughing like crazy, and I went back to see what was going on.

Her husband had been sitting there with the kids and it had blown like a leaf the whole length of the boat—the *Ranger* is sixty-eight feet long—and when his wife went back to tell him what happened everybody was buzzing about the ten dollar bill he'd grabbed out of the air.

And then they got really buzzing, you know, the kind of people who aren't too impressed with the whales anyway, who always say, "Oh, I've seen it all on TV."

Vet up-Cape had a whole body bag full of dead dogs to get rid of cause his freezer went out.

The dump up there closes early. So he gives the bag to some friend from P-town, who was passing through. They just heaved the bag in the guy's truck and he took it to the dump day, day after he got home.

Old lady, dump-picker, practically lives out there, she sees the bag, nice-looking bag, really really nice bag, luxury-class bag with a zipper.

She thinks, *Hey, must be something pretty special in there.* All these frozen dogs. Starting to go soft, dripping like they were drowned or something.

She raised the dickens with the head of the dump—the Administrator of the Sanitary Landfill ho ho—she convinced him there must have been foul play, all kinds of fancy abuse. She wouldn't let up on him.

So he gave in and shipped the dogs to a lab in Boston—they were all old, sick, euthanized—and he found out there was nothing wrong, no laws broken, zip. Except he got a bill for five hundred dollars.

Now he's trying to collect from the vet. The old lady don't have a cent, just junk she got from the dump.

Are we having a good time yet or what? Hey, want to see me get Robbie going? He's easy. I won't even have to try.

Hey, Robbie, that guy over there just said, "Fuck." He just used the word fuck. He said, "Fuck." Aren't you going to throw him out? Throw that fucking bastard out. You threw me out for saying, "Fuck." I'm the only person you ever threw out of here in your life for saying fuck. How come I'm the only one who gets shut off for saying one word. Everybody else does it. What's so fucking special about me? Why's fuck a bad word in my mouth and not in anybody else's? Hey, I know you think I'm a fucking jerk, but I'm still a fucking good friend of yours no matter what you fucking think.

Hey, that's my ice. Fuck you you fucking fuck. I fucking paid good money for it. Well, fuck you. I'm still your fucking friend though no matter what the fuck you do. And don't you fucking forget it.

Well, fuck him. You see what I mean? Nothing to it. You notice I didn't leave a fucking drop. I sucked that fucker down to the cubes. Well, fun's over. I'm getting the fuck out of here. Fuck him if he can't take a joke.

Hey, Robbie, you know I fucking love you. I'll be back tomorrow. You can count on it. You don't have to fucking worry. What the fuck, you worry! Okay, I'm going. Goodnight, Robbie. I'm going now. Goodnight, Robbie. Hey fuck you. Hey, Robbie, fuck you. ROBBIE, FUCK YOU and Me Tooooooo.

Doggy

This was back in the days when dogs ran free and men weren't women.

Addicted to adoption, Cindy was accustomed to attendant inconveniences, chiefly eczema, unexpected litters, aggravated neighbors, and eventual penury, as the town gentrified and owners of rogue canines began to get summonses to court in Orleans.

Her latest but one, Bad Boy, had been bad enough, upending garbage cans, rolling in offal and fouling the lawns up and down the street, but he had met his fate in a fashion both timely—before he could surpass the record of havoc compiled by the legendary Greeder—and so prodigal in its improbabilities that her mourning was greatly assuaged in the telling and retelling of it. Before that Muddy had been banally struck by a truck.

Her present nemesis, Doggy, a grinning mongrel, was so blessedly sweet tempered, clean, obedient and trusting, that she wondered if something might not be wrong with him, but then she decided that this was merely her karma, derived from former tribulations borne with fortitude, also perhaps to be taken as a warning against lapse from her heretofore inveterate benefactions.

Doggy sans collar had simply stepped in one day through her broken screen in the midst of her first peace in years. Bad Boy had finally faded into mere history, and on the entreaties of her long-suffering friends she was just mustering resolve to welcome no more pets, either lost or orphaned by people leaving town—she had succored sundry cats, ferrets, three goldfish named Ho Hum, two rabbits, a rooster, and a scurrilous parrot, as well as Abigail, an adolescent python she had segmented with a hedge clipper when, having climbed the rafters and descended into her hanging aviary, it swallowed her favorite finch Chirpy, then had the gall to be too contented or engorged to squeeze back through the bars.

Doggy proved to be a dream come true. He never hosted a flea, nor howled at moon or noon whistle. He did not puke nor vent vile winds, lose hair, nip children, nor mount stranger's legs. He shat only in distant neighborhoods and never attracted the attention of the Animal Control Officer, lately voted an elevated title and full-time writ and van with accoutrements to proscribe the unrestrained, the grim grimace and constant contusions and sutures on hands and face, his badge of the zealous pursuit of his duties. In short Doggy never caused Cindy the least discomfiture, of the usual sort, such as the time Muddy squatted on the wrong lawn and she looked back to see the shrieking owner flinging turds after her.

The former dog catcher, a gentle elder who whistled loose mutts to his hand, then strolled them home, had retired to his vegetable garden. He knew where every dog lived with the same native savvy imputed to the Post Office in delivering mail to wherever one had spent the night. Plastic bags and poop scoopers were coming into vogue, and the ritual sniffings of antic little breeds the size of cats provided a social matrix for their short-leash holders, the new wave of gay washashores.

Cindy by instinct was a cautious soul, as well as a dedicated solitary, and one of her fears—apart from her love of animals—was, if she didn't have at least one noisome cur in residence both as companion and deterrent, she might succumb to some man's—or woman's—seductions, and acquire a truly disadvantageous housemate.

The year of Doggy's advent she confidently took him with her on a rare expedition to Boston. A wisdom shared by certain susceptible citizens of Olde P-towne went thus: *Never leave Provincetown. Never. For any reason whatever, except inescapable in-*

*evitabilities such as births, marriages, deaths. It's a dangerous
world up there beyond the bridge, as all too many—or perhaps
too few—misadventures have famously testified.*

No sooner had they found a parking place than they happened
upon an old-fashioned escalator, an antique of sorts, last of the
last, with foot-polished, wooden treads and creaky, thunking in-
nards, a beautiful relic with sweet rhythms, no doubt about it, nor
any end of users cheerfully going up and down motionless as
mannequins, reading their newspapers or eyeing one another as
they passed with longing or aversion, wonder or indifference, ver-
itable ships in the night, sailing each toward his rock.

Doggy balked, for the first time in his life, at all Cindy's pleas,
commands, enticements and reassurances. He was simply scared
of the thing, and knew for a fact he never should have left home
himself. He dug in his claws and held back. So dear a friend of
Cindy was he that he wore no collar, and eventually, though it
hurt her heart, she pushed and hauled him after her by scruff and
rump. He panicked, resisted more and more fiercely, scrabbled
and fought, even bared his teeth in a silent snarl of hopeless
protest.

The relentlessly meshing treads caught a toe and tore it off to
the tune of their mingled screams, and left him with a mangled
left hind foot and limp, and her with a crippling need for redemption.

Doggy was never the same dog again. His friskiness was gone;
he no longer loved a frolic in the dunes, or on the beach; he hardly
strayed from his own front door, and abjectly piled turds on
Cindy's small patch of crab grass, lay around the house slit-eyed
like a cat and got fat.

But that was the least of it. He grew snappish, malign, mis-
trustful, utterly unforgiving. There evolved something in his eye
unbecoming to a pet, an unaccommodating gleam that gave him
sometimes the look of superior intelligence, of almost human

comprehension. Cindy suffered his surly maturing with a sick despair. He no longer slept on her bed, shrank from hugs, fled his
brush, growled at the door to be let out, let in, lifted his bad leg at
the stoop and pissed an evil-smelling stream of insatiable outrage
and choler.

No absolution could be won, no consolation found. Nothing
Cindy could do revived even a ghost of his late, panting, grinning
devotion to her. The whole human race appeared to be accursed
in his eyes, and she felt deeply, rightly at fault, writhed in frequent dream of a monstrous apparatus with teeth shredding them
both from the feet upwards, always mercifully waking before it
reached her chin.

When summer came again Doggy took to limping over to Commercial Street, sitting down in the middle of the sidewalk and
glaring balefully at passersby. He bit a tourist who bent to pat
him and the Animal Control Officer got bitten himself when he
came to take Doggy to the pound. As he still had no collar it cost
her seventy-five dollars to get him back, plus the license fee.

Thereafter he got hauled in regularly, which required a trip to
the pound one day, then to court another, and a fifty-dollar fine.
She and the judge developed a droll rapport. "Would you consider making Doggy the blessed gift of eternal sleep?" he once
ventured, having drunk too much coffee.

But it had already exhausted her moral reserve to collar, license and tie poor Doggy up, and still he got loose when she
wasn't looking. He could always outrun her, gimpy or not, bringing more sojourns in Orleans, and subjection to smirks, mirthless
digs, gross chortles from the courthouse functionaries. She was
going broke as well as mad, and had to quit drinking and dope.
Kerosene was up too, her rent took a jump, and she needed a new
pair of boots, plus a second job, with winter coming on and none
to be had, to say nothing of wear and tear on her wheels and
nerves.

Doggy

The situation became untenable. A cold Christmas approached, with her and Doggy housebound like Ethan Frome and his ruined love.

Bill Binjin had long been importuning Cindy—since the day they had met, to be exact—and for an equal length of time she had thought him an exemplary oaf. In lonely travail one day she allowed herself a personal plaint with him. Naturally he was roused by her helplessness, saw her relief in his cherished firearm that had never seen practical use, his well-maintained marksmanship, and his lack of a single scintilla of interest in why he was convinced that feeling was folly.

"You won't have to see or hear a thing," he said. "When you come back from your walk he'll be gone, no muss, no fuss. I'll garbage bag him with rocks and drop him off the wharf when the harbor master's busy. It beats grave digging."

Of course she could no more do this than she could give Doggy to the needle. Her sense of his former self had never dimmed. She knew she had no right to kill a creature that had sought her out, adored and trusted her, that she had made unfit to consort with the human race, that most certain agent of its every fortune in life.

But once on the scent Bill kept in full cry. Also, he was hard to keep out of the house, or get out, once in, having very fine dope, and nothing he wished to do more than dally all day with her. She found herself dressing a little less bagladyly, washing her beautiful, bushy, copper-blazing hair, and providing a beer or two, for the off-season called for just such delightful diversions, if only he had been someone else.

Meanwhile Doggy grew more and more intractable. She said to him one day, "You shouldn't hold a grudge too long. I couldn't help what happened." But nothing appeared in his cocked eye but the now-familiar evil gleam.

He had adapted to his limp, and no longer took on depredations that might require flight. Slyness reduced his need for speed. Knowledge of the enemy kept him from overt attacks. He slept till dusk in the coat closet, and spent the night Cindy knew not how, though she had unhappy suspicions. She caught a glimpse of him one foggy dawn coming home, sneaky, cautious, truculent as a raccoon, and she shivered.

A passing stranger on the street ground out, "That goddamned dog of yours!"

Bad luck does not last forever sometimes. Bev came to visit. She was a healer, and having heard Cindy's calvary set out to win over the wary beast.

Bill still insisted it ought to be shot. He and Bev hated each other at sight and had uproarious, sarcastic, insulting arguments, muddled by various stimulents. The philosophy of the world seemed somehow at stake, and their generalizations both embraced and excluded each other's bitterest sallies. In fact they agreed on nothing at all, not even allowing for the mutual, neutral ground of numbers. "You dim twit," Bill shouted. "There's a million different systems of math in which one and one are never two."

Bev made no effort to conceal her loathing of the man, his soul, his ideas and his gun, and hard upon his impatiently awaited departure one day said with contorted face, "I cannot tell you how I despise him, I really would like to rip his balls off with my bare hands."

After a particularly heated exchange Bill had said to Cindy, as if Bev were not there, "What a little twat she is!"

Bev spent much time persuading Doggy to come out of his closet, then kneeling beside him, where he lay keeled over on his side like a stunned ox, while she massaged his spine, working on each disc separately and humming an appropriate mantra, then shaping both hands over his whole corpus to relieve his aura of its toxins, a procedure Doggy seemed to tolerate or at least ignore, though now and then his tail went whack whack on the floor like a provoked cat's. Bill's howls of raillery reached unprecedented volume and contempt when Bev declared she could feel the edges of his violated chakras.

Cindy sat through these seances, as if she were not party to the issue, piqued that her guests paid her small heed, except as hostess and chair, through whom they skewered each other with unanswerable, snide ironies.

Strangest of all she awoke one morning to find Doggy asleep beside her bed, having not gone out the night before, and the next night, after a pitiable effort to climb upon her bed as in their green beginnings as a couple—he could no longer jump at all—she helped him up, and he slept at her feet the whole night without a single growl of dream.

Coming home unexpectedly early from work the next noon she heard a violent commotion in her bedroom, and thought Bill was beating Bev up, rushed to the rescue only to find a more equal sort of combat underway—one in which the man always loses—and quietly left the house, taking Doggy for a ride, his first since their bloody, hell-driven race back from Boston in time to catch the vet still in his office. Doggy sat in the front seat, and his tongue lolled out and his penis emerged from its prepuce like a scarlet tulip in spring.

Cindy was glad to see the last of Bev and Bill; so much cooing and clinging and lap-sitting she could not abide, and the worst—or the best—was, they took Doggy whom Bev could rightly claim to have cured, and whom in fact he did seem to prefer, when he was not making up to Bill, who with melting face and warped grin carried him to Bev's car and settled him comfortably on a blanket in the back seat.

And that, too sudden for assessment, was simply that. Bill's lease being up, he let his cheap place go and moved in with Bev in Boston, whence in due course came a call, not without its strains, from Bev herself, to say that she did not think Cindy had been quite honest with her, either about Bill's unspeakable predilections or about the preexisting basis of Doggy's disillusion with life itself. He had instantly wasted to a skeleton, and she had dropped him at the S.P.C.A. and fled, vets in Boston being costly as shrinks. Her call was largely a diatribe against Bill, to which Cindy could only murmur wanly, "I know, I know, I know."

Though to Cindy it meant everything—she did not care a fig for man or woman—Bev dealt with Doggy summarily, and devoted the rest of twenty uninterrupted, torrential minutes to the debacle with Bill, and his final expulsion from her apartment, thanks to her getting an even bigger bastard of a new boyfriend looking for lodging.

The moment Bev hung up, Cindy called the S.P.C.A. in Boston, but they had no record of any such foundling.

Bill, when she met him hunching the street in the spring, said sourly, "You cost me my place in P-town. It's not so easy to get back once you're gone."

A year later, dogless, beseiged by suitors, she got a summons from the Orleans District Court in reference to Doggy. Three months later she got another, with a warning of consequences for absence on the date named.

So, mystified, irritated, amused, up she went on the early bus, her car on blocks awaiting long-promised repairs, and in the last case on the docket, deep into the afternoon, was ordered to pay a fifty-dollar fine for Doggy's being seen unleashed on the street six months after he had presumably died in Boston. The Animal Control Officer, who well knew the lame renegade, had identified his slinking flight beyond the shadow of a doubt.

She scoffed and laughed, shrugged and pled, reasoned and railed more vociferously than was wise. The judge was not her familiar, empathetic pal, but a matter-of-fact stickler new to bench and venue. "Two days in jail if you prefer."

So she conceded the case, made arrangements to pay her fine

Doggy

over the next three weeks, and hitchhiked home in a downpour, eventually getting picked up by a ranting, racist lunatic, who frightened her so badly she got out in Wellfleet and walked two miles to a friend's house, and wound up spending the night at a friend of the friend's house, because the friend had brought a new boyfriend home for the first time.

Lying there on a lumpy couch impregnated with tobacco smoke and other smells she resolved to steel herself to accept and endure her next gift of a dog without demur, no matter how difficult or vile its eccentricities, and to lock her door when she went out.

Even years after she too had been priced out of Provincetown she was unable to find anything funny in Doggy's tale, alone among her many dog sagas, nor could she ever cease to lament the wonder he was the day he pushed his wide-grinning snout through her torn screen door.

For Carol, Susan, and Pat

The Throes

Coolan Scullars, born November 1958, died December 1987, due to an explosion in a transformer outside his childhood window, loathed fire, forbade cremation, at the end dithered, so alienated by his experience of life that he could name no place on earth he could stand to be buried, left his stymied friends to await the boats of summer.

Sedentary **Simon Fischer**, 40, stockbroker, prey to the perils of his era—overeating, anhedonia, disphoria, lacklove, despair—found in AIDS support groups the kinship he had vainly sought since college in sex, spent his last year attending the dying, reached his zenith ten days before his own death as one of six PWAs in a film about AIDS in Provincetown, standing alone upon the sea grass heaped beach, hands in pockets, face to the wind, exultant and free.

Africa Rox, 37, ghetto novelist, after an early succès d'estime, had faded into his exemplary marriage and milieu, drudge of the English Department, marooned in his color and love of men.

Lost to his gift, source and substance withered by academic strictures, he took solace in scholarship, planned a *Life Of Timoleon, Deposer of Tyrants*, for twelve years summered alone at Beach Point, castaway amongst the bars and his unpacked boxes of books, died in Amherst raving.

Quarious Lawson, 26, a sort of foundling, fed, sheltered, bettered and brothered by the staff of Cary's Cafe, who finally persuaded him to get tested, achieved his first mature conception of life in the form of a death sentence.

Traumatized, he reverted to boyish dodges and dreams, waned

precipitously, disappeared for a month of drinking and drugs, drowned of pneumonia in an unoccupied condo, infuriating his adoptive family, which, prepared to help him through condensed epochs of accelerated growth, chorused his epitaph through gritted teeth: *No One Dies of Pneumonia Anymore.*

John Conable, 34, Rhodes Scholar, author of two books on government, founder of a dance company, vice president of a consulting firm, bereaved of his ambition's greatest project, a revised international globe with ideal countries formed according to topography, economics, language and history, was eulogized as "a Renaissance man" by his longtime partner, **Sidney Hamil**, who died himself within the year, having wanted "only to be an ordinary person allowed to live out an ordinary life."

William Rowser, 33, praiseful of the virus that had turned him toward transcendence, bore his last days with fortitude, left his body by astral instinct at midnight of a full moon, eager for his next incarnation.

A gentle person of incredible spirituality and creativity, very unique in his versatility, fantastically accomplished in many art forms, especially poetry, painting, photography, video, sculpture, choreography, exquisite jewelry, dance, human relations, mime and macramé, he left an enlightened legacy of serenity and beauty.

Louis Laqueur, 43, in adulthood had striven for invisibility. At nineteen a virginal love in the navy, half-comprehended, naively confessed, had led to a medical discharge, when he refused to disavow his true feelings.

Subsequent years of psychiatry, of secret travail, of efforts to find eros in women, by sheer will to seize reasoned advantage, to yield to his own larger ambitions and interest—all proved futile before what he finally, reluctantly, concluded to be, in his case at least, an irrevocable writ of fate.

The death of his parents, whom he had successfully kept in the dark, fortified his resolve to forge through the rest of his life without further misadventure. He mastered the middle ground, grew obliging, self-effacing, objective, detached, sympathetic to everyone's troubles, no matter how ignominious or trite, always exuding a doctor's soothing manner and sanguine outlook, mild, reliable, grave and grey, never betraying his solitude.

He neither rose nor sank but held his own, neither ally nor adversary of anyone, throughout the factional vicissitudes of the mid '80s that racked his firm from top to bottom, became known to his grateful colleagues as an unshakable pillar of strength and sound judgment.

By the time he discovered Provincetown he had invested so much in his renunciation that he never felt at ease with a gay identity, dressed like a banker on a working weekend, avoided groups, evinced no interest in the world of camp and drag, succumbed only rarely and resignedly to furtive encounters with youths he paid and never saw again, indulgences which both dismayed and gratified him.

Certain summer acquaintances—he could not be said to have friends—exhorted him to quit the closet, dubbed him The Turtle, derided his outdated charade, condemned his selfish cowardice, but he faced them down pleasantly, without explanation or excuse, comfirmed in his course by the fact that his heart had never opened again after the disaster of first love.

Hector Smith, 50, epicure, misanthrope, valetudinarian, had habitually enjoyed ailments so many, nebulous and unremitting, that the few friends who could tolerate him, and the fewer yet whom he, in kinder moments, would occasionally suffer admittance to his cloistered domain, never dreamt that he was truly in extremis, and thus were baffled by the postmortem.

Born with a vivid sense of imminence, he could not abide the benighted, the bored, the banal, performed the least act of his perfectly devoted life with attentive meticulousness, fed his lilac-point Siamese Moonbeam and his autocratic Persian Thistledown with different spoons, kept their silver bowls brightly polished, changed their separate beddings once a month, groomed each with its own brush, was always in everything a martinet of precocious preciosity.

His faithful secretary, one Michael Patrick McGriffin, a personage of whose existence Smith's acquaintances were all equally ignorant, was revealed to be chief beneficiary and executor of the will.

The remains were consigned to Punta Gorda, Florida, their place of conception.

McGriffin's sole obligation was to have his elderly felines put to sleep, then to memorialize and inter them at opposite ends of the narrow garden where as carefree kittens they had leapt after butterflies, the private ceremony to be held at dusk the day of their quietus.

"What secretary? I didn't know he had a secretary. What on earth duties did he have?" Smith's friends asked each other.

Singular they were, to be sure. For the past fifteen years, at midnight on the first Monday of every month, Mick, a gorgeous specimen when Hector Smith first spied, interviewed and engaged him, had like Stealth incarnate been stealing in Smith's unlocked back door.

On tiptoe he would climb the dark stairs in the dark house, enter the dark bedroom and without dropping his pants open his fly and slowly, cloyingly bugger his perfumed employer, who feigned sleep in a variety of women's slips, shifts and nighties, face down, with a pillow bunched beneath his pelvis. No word was spoken, not so much as a sigh vented, nor at any chance proximity in the diurnal world was the least sign of recognition ever exchanged.

The rule of this routine was that the deeply breathing Smith must not be awakened, that Mick must reach and endure his climax without acceleration of thrust, without shudder, pleasure-paralyzed halt or sudden undammed spasm, the even flow of his semen to be undetectable in its subtle beginnings and end and prolonged until the final seepage of depletion, his phallus to be withdrawn only by its own detumescence, which in their early years not seldom issued in a titillating interregnum and second ravishment.

A quarterly check in the mail compensated Mick for what soon seemed not so onerous, nor so strange, a chore, one which in fact over the years he came to anticipate with a sort of admiring affection for his staunch fantasist, nor was it long before the remuneration became indispensable to him.

Thus, upon testing positive, Mick was thrown into a quandry, muddied somewhat by the thought that Smith was doubtless long since infected and could hardly benefit from a premature destruction of his peace of mind, or already knew and, loath to relinquish his accustomed pleasures, had simply ignored his condition.

And so Mick kept the silence of their bargain, and continued his now conflicted visits to the rose-covered bungalow behind Aunt Sukie's Way, but, increasingly beleaguered by illness and terror, he found they could be allayed only on Monday nights or in dreaming of these trysts, so that the prescribed constraints grew hateful to endure, sophistical to justify.

Eventually his plummeting health made him forget his employer's plight, and recognize his need for, even right to, a raise, given his long, loyal service, and the fearful cost of drugs.

Smith was away, as occurred each winter. The quarterly checks kept coming, as if Mick were on a retainer, though nothing had ever been stipulated about exclusivity.

It was in the fifth week of the latest of these recesses, and one week prior to his scheduled return, while Mick was mulling how to broach the issue of money—by phone? in writing? certainly not during the act, nor before, nor after—that Smith's obituary appeared in the *Clarion*, three uncommunicative lines of a reticence almost insolent.

The next day, amid a tumult of desperate despair and dumfounded bereavement for one whom after all Mick had hardly caught a glimpse of in years, he received by registered mail an incredible letter from the deceased's attorney, like winning a lottery he had neither played, nor known to exist.

Nor had he known of any cats, but in due course found himself one uncharacteristically soft May twilight alone in Smith's garden toting a cardboard box with the corpses of Moonbeam and Thistledown nestled together in it like a single, cumbersome pillow.

He was not feeling well. After the initial thrill of a confirmatory phone call and prompt receipt of a predesignated, preliminary installment on his inheritance, he had been taken by an intuition that a cure for AIDS was about to be found: how could it be otherwise?

He had decided to have a celebratory dinner, but as the hour approached he could think of no one he wished to treat and ended up at a solitary, corner table, dismally watching other couples regale themselves, while he sampled hors d'oeuvres and sipped a $175 bottle of champagne so dry it puckered his tongue and gave him a ringing headache before he had poured a second glass. The excitement, the exertion, the disappointment, all were too much. He never ordered an entree, asked for the bill, and was back home in bed by nine o'clock.

Rueful reflections had he that night lying there with the unheeded TV flickering in the dark room. Hector Smith, he now must needs admit, was the only true love he had ever had, certainly the least troublesome, the most durable and appreciative, the only one in the world Mick McGriffin would care to dine with. What could the man possibly have been like? He loved cats. Beyond that Mick hadn't a clue, only a deepening sense of mystery and regret.

He began to dig at the far end of the garden. Overhead the colorless sky seemed to brighten while shadows closed around the hedged-in yard. Instantly he lost his breath, though the ground wasn't hard. Every spadeful cost him a gruesome effort and he kept stopping to rest, hearing his own rasping pants in the stillness, feeling the clammy dank on his chill face, shivering in his own cold sweat.

Suddenly the world seemed to swarm. He leaned on the spade and looked up to quell his vertigo. The evening star emerged and danced. He swayed and nearly stumbled in, then stooped and carefully tipped the flimsy box, but both bodies slid as one. He stared down with resignation. Even to walk to the far end of the garden, much less dig a second grave, was simply more than he could do.

And actually the cats looked quite comfy together, sweetly sprawled and intertwined, little paws across each other's eyes. He felt elated that they would thus escape eternal solitude, felt sure his enigmatic benefactor would approve.

In fact the finicky cats had never got along. Clipped males too refined to unsheathe a claw, they had always disdained each other, did not cross paths, kept at exact and changeless remove, though always bound within sight of each other, emulating the exclusivity of their knowing owner, spent their entire existence watching each other's every move with unveiled abhorrence.

Mick was too tired to contrive obsequies, but simply covered them up, feebly as an old man trampled the mounded dirt, returned the spade to the shed, leaned against the locked door, trying to get his breath, his whole thorax arthritic, every bone pure ache.

Night had fallen; the stars had multiplied. At last he felt rested, no longer cold, or perhaps mercifully numb. In delirium he beheld a white beach with sickle-shaped palm trees, then a stately necropolis shining beneath a neighborly moon.

In the morning, his youthful heart leapt to vow, he would take a taxi to the Saab dealer in Hyannis, by noon in the car of his dreams be on the road south. Everything would be as it should be. He need only time his arrival in Punta Gorda for midnight next Monday.

Colvin Mutch, 26, perky little bitch, alcoholic, free-lance house-cleaner, who claimed to have been fucked in every bed in every guesthouse in Provincetown, quit drinking to quell his erotomania, didn't get tested because he no longer needed to brave knowledge of his true condition, enjoyed a few months of dwindling relief from frenzy, then shrank into a feckless gloom, never felt quite alive, never was quite himself again, until the night of wild abandonment he spent with two hunks he met at Herring Cove on the Fourth of July, who cajoled him into joining them in a few beers from their cooler, then cocktails at dusk on their deck, late dinner at Cary's, shirtless, sweat-slicked dancing at the A-House till one, pizza at Spiritus afterwards, followed by a tumid cruise of the immense, electrifying crush that jam-packed the whole street for three solid blocks, whereat, every last surrogate exhausted, back they trod arm-in-arm, him in the middle, to their borrowed house for a cognac, a valium, two poppers, and finally the big, round bed with all possible wants fulfilled at once, upon which single, superfluous, unforgiving folly he in bitter retrospect blamed his annihilation.

David Done, better known as Jessica Jordan, The Provincetown Queen, rare surviving female impersonator of his generation through which the plague had swept like a scythe, was killed crossing an eight-lane freeway north of Miami, behavior imputed to dementia of undiagnosed subacute encephalitis.

Pushing fifty, on stage he looked a lissome thirty in rhinestones and gave off sparks when he sang, "Take Me, I'm Yours."

He never mocked women; he perfected, he surpassed them. It was his highest kink to pick up straight men late at night, take them home to his dim abode and get laid without their ever guessing his sex. Unmasking fazed him not.

At noon he would blaze into the Old Colony wearing a skin-tight cowboy shirt with cream yolk, a black silk bandana, whipcord jeans tucked into blue boots with scornful spurs, and diamond studs in his ears. "Wake up, you jerkoffs. What is this here, a morgue? Suck those down. Tequila all round! You zombies don't get laid but once every five years! Suck those down! Bartender, hit them again."

Three rounds he force-fed in ten minutes, then was gone with a jangle, leaving a twenty dollar tip and hammered audience.

Graduate of S.U.N.Y. at Albany, he sang in the choir, enlisted in the Marines in 1961, and on his second tour of duty received a Purple Heart for wounds sustained at Hue in the Tet Offensive, upon discharge had played in clubs along the East Coast from Key West to Rockland, Maine.

Moe Mellard, 35, never turned a hair. "Who knows how long I've had it?" he said. "It's probably been there for years."

But no one else could believe it. He was the man to whom nothing ever happened, the man of no needs, and consternation struck admirers and enviers alike.

He had made millions in electronics, and retired early. The best of life lay before him, world travel, glamorous companions, all the adventures that perfect freedom could devise, yet some mysterious reticence, some secret melancholy held him in thrall.

The advent of leisure, after the sale of his company, had brought him a revelation—like an illness no one witnessed, from which he never recovered—that all lives disappoint, that all efforts at harmony are ultimately futile, that nature by nature is evil, the universe malign, that civilization must fail.

Though he loved to mingle and often entertained, no one knew his mind. With golden curls and ivory skin he looked like a vision of Phidias, the spirit of bold fortune, but within hid something unexpressed, the riddle of his charm.

But why should he not have wrung what sweetness he could from life before he lost his health? Too late, too late, nor can it matter, was what his manner said. He rallied the disconsolate. No griefs could conquer him. Single-mindedly circumspect, he remained idle, graceful, good-humored, unmarked and brotherly to one and all. People could not check their imaginations and, as he belonged to no one, each felt a personal, proprietary bond with him.

For a long time he fought off infections, so long in fact that some forgot or began to doubt he really had the plague, and only imperceptibly did his constitution seem to fail.

He affirmed, he repudiated nothing. Useless weariness won out at last. His viral ravages, left untreated, all meds foregone, reduced him in one week to a speechless vessel of comprehension. Glad to abandon his material affairs, he moved to a hospice house where his end hove into view.

At first he was relieved, freed of pain and choice, but then grim remorse grew in him like a horrid fetus. He sank into suspended animation, a sustained insomnia, alone, beyond physical sensation, stricken with perfect consciousness.

From a dimensionless point above the bed he could see the wasted shell of what had once been Moe Mellard, inert except for his eyelids, which blinked in fluent code. He could clearly see, clearly hear, his friends coming and going, tending him, periodically confirming that he still lived.

He realized their ignorance, their awful contingency.

It was as if he must make a Herculean effort to square the circle, knowing full well it could not be done, yet must be done, lest all be virtual, never achieve the real.

He understood at last what hinged on him, how he alone must save the human enterprise, defeat despair, communicate that victory and fly home to the sun. Everything depended on the message his eyelids unceasingly sent unnoticed and unread.

His heart broke, for all his knowledge, all his stoic acquiescence, all his long constraint, had availed nothing, and amid the ineluctable agony he had denied himself in life he died.

Op Ed

As everyone knows but no one says, Sex is the great human conundrum—worse than death, which has no ultimate answer, but merely bedevils us into reconciliation. But we need not die of sex. Sex can be harnessed, and put to good uses.

The second great problem—our time and place being the most advanced in history—is the human ego, its low esteem of itself.

The key to both is masturbation, not only a social boon but a pure and simple pleasure available to all, with proper training in mental and physical techniques, which should be taught in school, starting in kindergarten or earlier, before children acquire the prohibitions of religion, vulgar prurience or prudery.

It is the most immediate answer, one nature has provided, even, one may say, urged on us, a resource universally known, but censored, slandered, suppressed by civilization so-called.

One loves the self above all else, and regardless of what idealistic philosophies may propound, one should. And this is good, not bad. Conceive the consequences if one loved others as much, and vice versa. Life would be perpetual flight from fiends all too many and grisly to envision. Let us free ourselves once and for all of these primitive dreams!

Let me state unequivocally that ill-intentions should not be attributed to opponents of masturbation.

Only they have not yet made the right connections—with themselves!

Masturbation is a thoroughly engaging, productive, harmless pastime, and a healthy one. Everyone of course has at least some experience in the practice of self-love, and not few must recall times when lack of same led to risky or downright dangerous surrogates.

Adequately explained and promoted as public policy, this activity would put a prompt end to prostitution, and curtail suicides of solitude or lack of reason to live.

Self-love regularly, faithfully employed, will make people better beings, more contented, independent, moral and proud, with a higher regard for themselves, and therefore more respect for others.

Dutifully, diligently conducted as needed, it would greatly reduce the dolors of amorous loss as well as the rate of murder, mayhem and accidents of inattention and daydream. Industry would prosper.

Nature is not seldom our deadliest enemy, while youth, being least resistant to impulse, ignorant of past and future both, quicker in defiance, abler in strength, apter in occasion, to make fateful or fatal submissions, the accelerated advance of age must be deemed the prime principle in developing desirable lifestyles.

Nor are there, nor have there ever been, nor can there ever be, just prohibitions against such initiatives, the first function of the free homo sapiens acting in accord with its own untrammeled interests and will, enjoying its most fundamental volition, not to mention redemption of time otherwise lost to unfulfilled distractions.

The dignity of civic spirit adheres to accomplished self-love, and honor should attend it, though envy need not, for success in private arts cannot be conflictive, but must rather conduce to the general harmony, in which one and all have equal chance, roles, and responsibility to participate.

Democratic values would flourish, joy and kindness reign.

Outcomes

I counted on them. I always thought of them as my lifeline, my refuge, my stable family in the wilds of Minnesota. I would go visit them when my latest love affair went smash or when I was drinking too much and afraid I would never paint again. Or when I got convinced my life was going to waste. Which was about once a year. They always patched up my confidence and resolve and sent me back into the battle to get butchered again.

The truth is I never could have stuck it out without them. They were also always urging me to get out of P-town and find a husband. Very gently, very tactfully. They didn't push it, they were nice about it, but I was never in any doubt about what they really thought. But they understood about compromise, about doing what you have to do to get what you want, about making sacrifices, keeping the faith and so forth.

That was what I admired the most about them, that was what their marriage was based on, in exactly the same way the single life and no children was the foundation of mine. If I wanted to be a painter I had to paint. It was either marry a millionaire or stay single and skip motherhood. I don't say I didn't have plenty of second thoughts and bolt uprights in the middle of the night.

My sister called me yesterday. She was weeping. Her husband left her. All this hit me right out of the blue. I was jealous of her. I always adored him because he was so self-reliant and trustworthy. And practical. He's a forest ranger. He can do anything with his hands. He built their house, he's the strong rugged type. He never said much, but he always seemed good-humored and happy with my sister.

I didn't know they were having trouble, they never breathed a word to me.

She said in the last year they'd gone from bickering about everything to not speaking at all. She finally got him to go to a marriage counselor with her. The guy must have been an idiot. You never know who's out there in the yellow pages. The guy said there was just nothing he could say. There was nothing to be done. They simply had incompatible objectives in life, never mind that they'd been married for twenty years.

So then she decided it must be some aftereffect of his upbringing. Maybe that was why he hadn't wanted children of his own. His father died young of cirrhosis, his mother was very promiscuous for a while before she got remarried to a guy who resented every minute she spent with her kids.

Anyhow, she made him listen to some tapes by Adult Children of Alcoholics, and suddenly all he wanted was to get out of the marriage. Said he wanted his own space, wanted to do his own thing. Overnight he became this New Age person. He got an earring, let his hair grow. He started hanging around in town. They live out in the woods all by themselves. He said he couldn't stand the solitude anymore. She said he was so different she wasn't even sure if she still liked him.

One day they were fighting over some little nothing, and he went in his workshop and came back waving a letter he'd written to an old girlfriend and never sent back in the days when he was courting my sister.

It said he'd met this nice woman, but she demanded more commitment than he really could give. He says, "See this? See this? I knew it all along. I knew I was right."

My sister wanted kids, he hadn't. They'd discussed it for years. It was a very difficult decision for her of course, but she'd made the sacrifice for his sake. And most of the time she'd been happy, and thought he was too.

And now he's gone and she's fifty years old and living alone out in the woods.

I just have a hunch. He'll find a younger woman and start a family, now he's old enough to figure out what he's been missing. And my sister will be the one who let him in on the secret. Took her twenty years of course.

And he'll probably be a good father too. And my sister can't change. Into what? She's too set in her ways. And now she's sort of leaning on me, and I don't know what to say to her. "Get a dog? Move to P-town?"

Cranberries

You remember Nolan Lunday. Everyone knew Nolan. Well, after he died Leota and some of his friends got together a book of his poems, and had them printed, a little book, you know, edition of a hundred. Some of them were very good. I didn't even know he wrote, no one did really.

So when I went to buy one they were all sold out. Every six months or so I'd remember and say to myself, I've got to get one of those. And I did finally.

Actually I'd just spent about three days cleaning Munmer's house, mountains of his accumulated junk and mess, dogshit and dishes from the month he moved in. Unbelievable.

Since I was in the neighborhood, when I got done I dropped in to see his widow. I said, I'd like to buy one of Nolan's books, they were like $5.95.

She said, "Oh, you can have one."

I says, "Oh, I want to pay for it."

She says, "Well, I've got two or three or four around here somewhere," and she looked all over the house, and couldn't find a one, and then I started to walk around too, and I noticed one sitting right out there in plain sight on her bookshelf, Nolan's bookshelf I guess you could probably say.

But she wouldn't take any money. I said, "Well, you gave me something, I'll have to give you something. I'll bring you some cranberries some day. I have a beautiful, secret little bog nobody knows about."

She says, "Oh, cranberries! Cranberries were what killed Nolan. He was crazy about cranberries. He died picking cranberries. I still have some from the day he died. The police gave them to me."

And she went to the refrigerator and brought back two bags—he'd been dead about two years—but they were empty. There was not a single berry left, but the bags were still there in her refrigerator. She was not a young woman. I mean, they were both in their eighties when he died.

But that brought how it happened all back. He'd gone out to pick cranberries, but he couldn't find any, or at least none to his liking. So he drove into P-town. Maybe he just wanted to go to the O.C. and have a few belts, or he changed his mind, but anyway at some point he went to the A&P and bought a batch of cranberries that he switched into a couple of his own bags.

Which got found with him in the car pulled over by the side of the road when he had his heart attack on the way home.

The reason his poems got published in the first place was because his wife discovered them in a cubbyhole in his desk when she was going through his effects. She didn't know he wrote poems. He never told her, never told anyone. I guess he didn't think it was worth mentioning.

Anyhow in due course I picked some cranberries and Leota and I took them over to her house. She said, "Oh, thank you. How nice. Would you like something to drink?"

So we said, "Well, yes."

She said, "I don't have anything in the house, but he always had things stashed all around here." She started to hunt around. She knew where to look, and in about two seconds she found a pint of whiskey under the sink.

So we sat there eating raw cranberries out of a bowl and drinking Nolan's whiskey. That was really something.

God Knows

I told her I had cancer. Well, I wasn't thinking clearly. Of course she was horrified. I thought it would put an end to her interest in me, her attachment, her hopes, whatever. I thought she'd drop me like a bad debt—I told her it was prostate cancer, God knows why. I guess I thought she'd be repelled.

When that didn't put her off I told her the cancer had spread to my testicles. I was just too embarrassed to tell her the truth. I always enjoyed her company, she sort of built my ego up. I wasn't used to that from women, it was very soothing, very strange, sort of like being a hermit, but then I finally just decided I wanted more life. I just wanted to get rid of her. Or at least be out of reach of her icky fingers. I was sick of the charade, but I didn't want to hurt her feelings, and I didn't want to come out to her either, God knows why, maybe because in the back of my mind somewhere I'd actually been harboring the thought of trying to go straight with her—can you imagine?—which made me all the more ashamed. Or maybe I was just tired of getting shit on my dick. Well, small chance in this day and age. It's all too complicated to explain.

So then she read Merck's Manual, which has all the symptoms and prognoses and treatments of every disease there is—believe me, it doesn't pull any punches, you'd think it wasn't real people in question—and now she's an expert on the entire genital region of the male. I had to buy one myself—they're not cheap either—and now I have to study half the night to keep up with her, not to mention all the lies I have to tell about going to Boston for chemo and radiation, and how am I feeling? and isn't it wonderful I haven't lost any hair yet!

The fact is, she's some sort of a ghoul I'm beginning to think. How can she still like me with all these diseases? Don't tell me it's true love, I know better. It's just perverse, she's like a steel trap too. Of course prostate cancer and tumors of the testes have nothing in common, they don't turn into one another, ever, and she called me on it. It's frightening how much I know about this stuff now, it's all pretty grisly and depressing. I had to say, "Well, it's coincidental, they're unrelated, they just presented at the same time, I'm just doomed is all."

She says, "Oh, no you're not. We'll fight, we'll fight them both, and we'll win." She's all hyped up. I've never seen her so exuberant. She's almost glowing, actually I've never seen her so beautiful. Like a fool I made the mistake of telling her that. Not a shrewd move. Well, it's nice to be able to make a person happy with one little line, even if it's true.

I was thinking about having it spread to my pancreas, or pop up on my kidney or liver, that's usually fatal, but then I realized how much I'd have to learn. Just skimming those sections made me sick. There's no consideration for the reader at all in that book. None. I'd never open it if I didn't have to. Now I'm beginning to think I'd better go into remission quick, but where would that get me? We'd have to have a big celebration. Frying pan to fire. All my efforts gone for what?

Of course I could pretend to fall in love with Jacqui. I'm sure she'd go along, but that would really seem crass, ungrateful after all she got me through. I may have to marry her after all, or screw her at least.

No, no, just joking, but I'm really getting a bit desperate these days, I have to admit. I thought I was taking a sort of graceful leave of her, like I was going off to die in solitary grandeur, like a dignified old cat, except I'm still here. I thought it would be an easy exit—like committing suicide—and then there's nothing to worry about ever again. Well, let me tell you, it was only the beginning, Buttercup.

She's determined to nurse me. She comes around with food, I'm getting fat, she brings all these pamphlets with homeopathic progaganda. I keep saying, "Plain old ordinary Western medicine's good enough for me." And she says, "Well, this is just a supplement. You should be attacking these neoplasms in every way possible."

Neoplasms! And I have to read the damn stuff because she quizzes me on it, like urine therapy? She wants me to try it. Actually, it sounds quite convincing. But am I going to start drinking my own piss when I'm not even sick? Of course, I've begun to worry that all these lies, all this mental simulation, is going to get me sick. I mean, pretending to have cancer—two cancers—is that any way to keep your health?

It's a muddle, I admit. Well, fall will come and save us both. She'll go her way, I'll go mine. God knows why I should even care. Half the time I think she's just playing along. The whole thing's too crazy to believe. I don't look sick, do I? Do I? She probably knows I'm gay. How can she not know? She probably took it for granted from day one. She probably thinks I've got HIV and don't want her to know. She's just trying to be a friend.

Thanks for listening. She's been my only confidant since I got here last spring. I've been totally dependent on her, and now all the things I need to tell her I can't.

Maybe I should say it's AIDS after all, that I've been too embarrassed to tell her. Like it came from the blood supply or some prostitute down in Tijuana, and I was afraid she'd think I was gay. Maybe that's the way out. But why should that get rid of her? She'll just buy a lot of condoms and start reading up on protease cocktails.

Or maybe I could say I just don't want to talk about it, I'm too sensitive, I just can't face it anymore. I'll tell her she's my only respite. We'll act like I'm in perfect health. We won't even mention it, it'll be like a contract, like a bond, between us. We'll go around like everything is incredibly normal. But everything we do, everywhere we go, will be like a ritual occasion to keep my mind off my cancers, it'll have a beautiful, tragic undercurrent. Like endless farewells. We'll make a stunning couple, with something latent, something potent, something otherworldly, untouchable about us.

The trouble is I'm starting to feel like a disease myself. Like I might be contagious? I know cancer's not catching, but I hate to leave the house. To tell you the truth, half the time I'm scared half to death, and I haven't even got her to talk to about it.

Actually I don't know if she wants sex or not. We have this delicate little tip of the lips kiss at the end of each evening, not even moist. She's dry as a bone. I always sort of fantasize. I opened my eyes once, and she opened hers. I closed right up again, so I don't know what she did. Maybe she's a Lesbian. What a tangle. I never could stand women.

The News

Remember when Roland Foxrood was here? I was the one who got him invited. He was a wonderful writer, the last of my adolescent gods, after the immortals, Conrad, James, Stephen Crane, and Ford Maddox Ford. Among the living my first love was Hemingway, but he shot himself; the second was Flannery O'Connor, but lupus got her; finally there still breathed and walked upon the earth only my third, and last hero, that paragon of uninflected eloquence and implacable plots, Roland Foxrood.

I read all his early books when I was at the Iowa Writers' Workshop. He didn't have the kind of acclaim he deserved, but who does? And he was famous enough to make a decent living, by which I guess I mean he never had to teach. All his books were still in print. This was back in '81, the year before he died. He had a walk-up on the top floor of a run-down building on the wrong side of Beacon Hill in Boston—tiny, I heard later—he wrote on the kitchen table, and got himself taken out to dinner a good deal. By women, I mean. He was legendarily handsome and charming. At one time. He was the sort of man—according to another famous novelist I won't name—that you daren't leave your wife alone with for one moment. If you stepped out to get more beer, when you came back he'd be fucking her in the broom closet. He was an expert on the sexual habits of a certain class, a bit more Bohemian, more leisured perhaps, than the denizens of John O'Hara's realm. He never married or cohabited or had kids. He spent a lot of time in London. He was fifty-seven the November night he got off the bus in a blustery wind, with only me there to meet him. He didn't even own a car. I was twenty-five, and still nearly as green as the day I learned to read, so it didn't seem all that odd—distinguished author arriving by bus, the sole passenger, sitting up beside the driver, smoking a verboten cigarette, with one battered suitcase held shut with a belt, and not in the least a recent shave. But a thirst! Oh, yes, pizzazz and a thirst.

Well, I was gratified to oblige. Those were the good old days, when it was well known that the main fare of genius was alcohol, and the solvent of all obstacles more alcohol.

I walked him to the Work Center, having wrestled his suitcase away, and got him settled in the bottom floor of the barn, barren as a barracks, without any amenities. The boiler and furnace, which also served the two top floors, rumbled and roared behind a partition. He meandered around like a perfunctory cat, glancing once at everything from an approximate distance, pronounced it all "very comfortable."

When we went back out, about thirty seconds later, the suitcase was still standing in the middle of the room where I had left it, him having ignored all my efforts to discern where he wished it disposed. I should write a novel about that suitcase. There was certainly little in it. "A snarled suit and one shoe," he said when I asked.

Thus began the visit of Rolly Foxrood. I enjoyed him immensely, and tried not to worry. His last three books had been dull things, dead ground retrudged, the reviews hedged with respect, regret, rue. He was like a scuttled ship with flags flying. No matter his physical distress, even before his first drink of the day, he laughed loudly, hoarsely, spasmodically, as if life were continuous, outrageous jokes, and somehow, wherever he was, at least in my ken, he contrived to make it so.

How to reconcile this wreck with his earlier works I knew not. He was frivolous about everything except having a good time. He abandoned his reading of an old story after four pages, declaring irritably, "I can tell it better than that," and did so in about two minutes flat with headlong zest, and then applauded himself for his considerate treatment of his large, expectant house, concluding, "None more pitiable than the victims of prolixity," and set out for the drink table, waving his audience on like a platoon leader going into battle.

At the party afterwards, he stayed till the end and became slyly obnoxious, the most arrogant man imaginable. He insulted everyone present, mocked writers who had been at the Work Center previously, calling one of the most popular, who had just won the Pulitzer Prize, "a flat tire." He was the lewdest thing you ever saw, and used the foulest language. He was funny too. God, he was funny. And he propositioned every female there; you couldn't keep his hands off them, and when they demurred he commented unfavorably on their anatomies. When with much trepidation I remonstrated, he grinned good-naturedly and said, "They know I don't mean anything. But why have they all got such fat asses and mean tits."

He was supposed to read manuscripts, but after that night no one was willing to go near him. Partly this was a matter of mere chance. In another year, with a different group of Fellows, he might have been lionized.

In any case he was not dismayed. Work of any sort was not what he wanted. All he wanted was to drink and laugh and get somebody into bed with him.

He wound up holding court at a back table at the Windbourne Cafe, where the drinks were cheap, the food and coffee bad, and business slow. His disciples were few—Joanna and me—but faithful. We spent three days with him, morning, noon and night.

He was a horrible homophobe. He would rant, "Look at that faggot. This town's full of faggots. There's nothing but fucking queers here. Look at that fairy. There's another one."

We couldn't shut him up, he was too drunk, too gleeful, too august and dissuasive. Fellows happening in were disgusted or indignant, and kept apart, so we had him to ourselves, more or less, along with serendipitous bystanders.

Drawn toward our boisterous pit, one bleary character, when introduced, exclaimed, "You're not Roland Foxrood. I met him once. You're not him."

"Neither are you," said Rolly. "Sit down. Have a drink."

"I don't drink with imposters," said he, and walked away to the bar.

We laughed and laughed and kept laughing helplessly.

He looked like a corpse all right, a shambling hulk, a shell, with red and purple, mottled face and dirty shirt. What sense had he of himself? I do not know. He seemed genuinely perplexed that Joanna would not go to bed with him. He actually appeared to grow fond of her, and she liked him well enough, admired him to the stars, and rarely let herself get riled.

"If you didn't huff and wheeze like a walrus," she said. "You're going to kill yourself."

He chain-smoked, and there were long intervals of interrupted talk while he coughed. Joanna was determined to get him to read her novella and favor her with his thoughts.

"Bed first," he would say, "and then we'll see."

I had nothing to show, and would not have bothered him for the world. I was working on my first novel then, which never got finished, anymore than my second or third. In the ten years since, I have made many beginnings and middles, but as yet no ends, and sometimes I think of Rolly Foxrood as a bad omen.

Joanna simply brought her manuscript one morning to breakfast, which included plenty of rum with the coffee. "No grappa in this hick town," he grumbled.

As soon as the waiter had cleared the table she took her 125 pages out of its folder and lay it before him. "Read," said she.

He gave her an evil glower. I snickered. He snorted, grinned at me and began to laugh uproariously. We laughed and laughed at a gallop—I galloped, she galloped, we galloped all three. There is no escaping literature, never for one moment, for such as us.

There we sat past noon, Joanna and I at shoptalk. Oblivious, he read and grimaced and nodded and muttered and shook his head, glancing up to glare at her from time to time, while we all made the rum of the world go down.

We ate a little lunch, and I went home to bed. Returning toward dusk, I found them in animated exhaustion, talking as if they might go all night. I ate a sandwich and left them to their ardors.

Later she said it was the most harrowing day of her life, the most shocking and enlightening. She learned more from him than all her past workshops combined, and I was mightily gratified.

"Now," he had said then, "bed!"

"Don't be silly," she said.

"You owe me," he said.

"You were just doing what you were supposed to do," she said. "Besides I don't fancy you. I'm afraid you'll have a heart attack."

"That's the way I want to go," he said.

This wrangle lasted till the end of his stay. He never despaired, never gave up, thought she ought to be honored, with which opinion she was staunch to concur.

At his departure I couldn't get him a ride to Boston. He was too smelly and gross for the women, too disparaging for the men.

I carried his suitcase to the 7 A.M. bus, and put him aboard with a pint of rum. He said goodbye casually. I don't think I made much impression on him, though he had lambasted me from head to toe for my lack of production. I was amazed to realize how deeply sorry I was to see him go.

About a year later his obituary stunned me in the *Globe*. I went out and got a *Times*. There was little I had not known, except that he had never gone to college. He had said his father was a working stiff. "The old man was glad I was out of that. I never said it to him, I would never say it to anyone but someone like you, but the fact is it's taxing work."

I felt terrible. It felt like the end of something, what in retrospect proved to have been my youth. In those days I expected to write and publish books, and make at least a little money. So did a lot of people, but it didn't turn out that way.

Several years later Joanna came back to town. She was still revising her novella. I was doing clerical for an insurance agency in town. My father had been in insurance, and I had simply gravitated toward the familiar, while I worked up my courage to move to New York.

We went to the Windbourne to reminisce. The place was gentrified and utterly different. We wouldn't have raised a voice. She told me her sequel, which I had not heard before.

"I never told you this?" she said in disbelief.

She had gone back about a week after he left to apologize to the waiters. "I'm so mortified, it's all my fault, I'm the one who kept bringing him here," she said. "I'm responsible. I was afraid nowhere else could stand him. I really apologize."

They had looked at her like she had two heads. They had no idea what she was talking about.

Finally she said, "You remember, the grizzled old geezer at the back table who gave everybody such a hard time."

"Oh, him," they said, "you mean the bitchy queen."

Joanna and I laughed and laughed askance, starting up and starting up again, unable to keep stopped, our eyes meeting only briefly, shamefacedly, then shying away, appalled, horrified, chagrined.

Easter at the Old Homestead

June's the only woman living there. All the rest are men. Reprobates to the core, each and every one. Trisker and Tom True and Rad the Bad and Jimmy Zee and Turtle and god knows who all else on any given night.

The day before Easter Sunday June says, "Tomorrow morning we're having an Easter egg hunt."

They all thought that was pretty funny. They thought she was joking.

She said, "We always used to have an Easter egg hunt when we were kids. You're nothing but kids yourselves. Second childhood. Well advanced. You'll love it."

They just scoffed. They says, "Come on, June, get real."

She says, "I've been nostalgic lately, living with all you galoots. I always used to love those Easter egg hunts. My mother always made it special for us. I never cared for Christmas, I don't know why."

"Don't knock it," says Rad. "No Christmas, no Easter." He's the pedantic one, always talking about first causes, sufficient causes, efficient causes, why things happen or don't happen. He never got over his education.

She kept talking up her Easter egg hunt. They were having their usual Saturday night bat. She's drinking right along with them. If the truth be known she could probably drink them all down. She's a lot younger and a lot less played out.

About midnight after they toddled off to bed June went around outside the house with a flashlight, finding good hiding places. She'd spent about fifty-dollars, and she spared no effort, crawling

into the rose bushes, under the steps, ferreting out the most un-
likely or inaccessible spots she could think of.

About noon the next day she rousted them out. "Time for your
Easter egg hunt. Time for your Easter egg hunt. Everybody up."

They just pulled the covers over their heads and groaned.

"Get up, get up, you lazy-brains. Rise and shine. I already let
you sleep way past any self-respecting resurrection."

Get up, get up, get up! Come on, come on, come on, boys, up!
Up! Up!

I won't repeat the things *they* said. She kept yelling and pulling
their covers off. After a while they didn't answer, they didn't even
open their eyes anymore. What could they do? They just lay there
and took it.

Finally she yells, "These aren't exactly Easter eggs, you know!
These are little nips."

She'd bought a whole, huge assortment of fancy stuff, stuff you
wouldn't ordinarily drink on a dare—Amaretto, Sambucca, Coin-
treau, Pernod, peach schnapps, Kahlua, Chartreuse. Great stuff
for a morning after, start of a really legendary binge.

What could they do? It was Sunday morning. There wasn't
even any beer in the house, not a drop of anything, just the smell
of coffee, and her beating on their eardrums with a soup kettle
and a metal spoon.

They rolled out of bed in their underwear and stumbled out-
doors. It was a bright day. By that time word had got around, and
a whole gallery of spectators was awaiting them.

They looked pretty sheepish, but June got her Easter egg hunt.
Quite a great revel it grew into. Everybody joined in. She'd hid-
den some of the nips so well they never got found, and sometimes
you still see people poking around the house at dawn on a Sunday.

It'll be interesting to see if this becomes an Easter tradition,
like the Bum's Picnic. Remember that? Food and drink and dope

enough to go till dark, and music and dogs and babies and kids, a whole big family shebang. Then it got renamed the People's Picnic, sign of the times, and then we had several springs running of heinous weather, and the event never got out of the bars again, and faded away entirely, I don't know if anyone even noticed, or missed it, or remembers, whatever.

The Last Straw

There's a volunteer at the Support Group, she's gay, she's manic-depressive—she quit drinking at least—she was out on the West Coast for years, tried to kill herself no end of times. She was always being hauled to the hospital and pumped out. She's got razor scars on her neck and wrists.

So she was trying to put some meaning in her life with AIDS work. She was sitting with Jonas Freeman every afternoon. One day when she was flushing his catheter she drew some blood and injected herself.

"So," I says, "you finally succeeded. I suppose congratulations are in order. Patience, too, what with all these new drugs. I hope you don't change your mind."

She laughed. She used to be so dour she was practically comatose. I'd never even seen her smile before.

She said it took her just twenty-four hours to regret it. Of course she tested positive right away. *In*side of three months. Now she spends all her energies trying to guard her health. She says she's starting to enjoy life for the first time since she was a child, doing things she never did before. She's so full of love she's dripping. For everybody, she says.

I asked her why she did it. She said it was the last straw. I couldn't quite follow. Apparently there was a very nice looking guy that went by Jonas's window every afternoon at four o'clock, and Jonas got a crush on him.

She'd crank the bed up, they'd sit there waiting for him. It was the high point of his day, the one thing he had to look forward to. They'd talk about what the guy was wearing, what he wore the day before, did he look tired, was he sad, was he going to work, was he single—he was obviously gay, he had very good taste in clothes—what was he like? They invented a whole life for him, parents, family, lovers, Boston, New York, escape to P-town, everything.

And Jonas, you understand, was very ill. This was all that was keeping him going. And for herself she didn't care about anybody. She'd been alone for years. She couldn't care about anything, is what she told me. She kept saying, "He was at death's door and he was falling in love. And he didn't even *know* the guy!"

Maybe that's what she meant by the last straw. Anyway Jonas is dead, and she's . . . come alive with HIV.

You Tell Me

Littler this? Start your day off right! When's a better time of day? You tell me. Nobody's around, nothing's open, can't be any trouble if there's no people. Just sit here in the shade and look at the bay.

Be a scorcher. Lotta bad vibes sizzling through that ozone. Industrial sabotage is what that is. This whole spit is pitted with septic, like a bad tooth. Sea's toxic too. I eat nothing out of that bay. Nothing from the A&P either, if I can help it. Mercury, fertilizer, insecticides. Vegetables injected with cancers. When's the last time you saw a wild animal? You tell me. They're hounding the whales to death.

I threw away all my money. I got rid of it. Filth, every penny. My kids are grown, I don't need anything. What's to want? You tell me.

I don't say these things, it doesn't pay to go against the powers that be, but AIDS has the look of a man-made disease. So's that Ebola. Diseases rip-snorting out of where the jungle used to be. The medical profession's out for profit, bad as the lawyers and politicians. What's the use of working? You don't get paid unless you own the money. Where's the democracy here? What's the point of voting? You tell me. I won't give the bastards the satisfaction.

They don't tell us anything but lies. The comets are coming, the sky is blinking with UFOs, but they keep saying everything's ok, if we just bail out the bankers. They're trying to put us to sleep. It's all one big cover-up. You see those high tension lines running into town? You can hear'um hum, you can hear'um crackle, see'um spark in the mist at night. Now they're going to bombard us with micro-magnetic waves, stick a tower on top of the Monument, and tax us for it too. Leukemia, lymphoma, brain tumors, blood pressure, deathoma. What would you expect? It all started with the billions old Joe Kennedy bootlegged from Prohibition. He loved that Hitler. Who d'you think brings the drugs in? The C.I.A.? National Security? You tell me.

Well, we've still got our healths, God knows how. Lotta salts in the drinking water. How's your ticker? Mine's fine, the doctor says. He says I worry too much. Wouldn't you? I live with my mother. I'm the only one of the family who can still put up with her conventional ways. She's a fanatical housekeeper, scrubs everything down all day long, and the minute she gets done she treats herself to a cup of tea and then starts all over again. She's always too tired to sleep, so she crochets doilies and antimacassars till dawn blows, and she rolls me out of my dreams into this ridiculousness. The sideboard's piled up with white lace like a morgue, never even used yet. I don't dare move a muscle. I can't smoke indoors. She thinks I don't drink anymore. Why do I stay here? You tell me.

Silence

Who knew of his incredible works? He never published, never won a prize, laid no claims at all. Few knew he wrote. An immigrant here, he was hardly known to exist.

Alone he produced a prodigious literature in American English, then a second, depicting a fabulous world in an Esperanto of his own device. He wrote in both realms poems, plays, stories, histories, novels, travelogues—though he rarely left his desk—philosophies, pyschologies, journalism, limericks, jokes, rhymes, puns, neologies as yet unnamed, but as each part of his dual design came to perfection he burnt it. Doubtless this monk's intimacy with the coffin sustained his transparent spirit, but some of us—mere hacks and blurbers were we to him—counted him an utter cipher.

All negatives, he revealed no vices, led an eventless life, never laughed nor cried, knew the meaning of neither triumph nor defeat, never had a lover or friend, seldom spoke, closed his eyes at cameras, never danced, drank or savored sentiment, rose at dawn, wrote till dark, never napped or got sick. A biographer would suffer.

Yet the fact remains of his unheard of works and the supreme design conceived to express everything real and ideal, which is barely begun, not because of what he destroyed—he forgot nothing and carried the whole in his head—but because there was too much; always and ever the battle was lost, moment by moment, though he redoubtably toiled till his suicide at ninety.

That day, his infirmities having grown past coping with, he burnt his notebooks, unfinished fragments, would-be posthumous leavings, the thousand letters he never sent, a selection of which might have shed light on his aesthetics of individuation.

It was a windy day and the faithful incinerator wouldn't ignite, but a boy came by and lit it for him, then helped him back into his house, looking with wonder on the squalor of age.

When he was alone again he lay down and, as occurs in his first autobiography (the true one) put in his mouth the cyanide he had kept by his bed since his fiftieth birthday. He crossed his wrists and ankles, dropped his eyelids, assumed the rictus sardonicus and bit the capsule.

A death cast would have shown an ordinary face.

The Wages of Faith

I, my whole family, we go back a long way here. We're like the Mayflower Portuguese. We went to St. Peter's from Day One. All of us. Everyone I knew. Neighbors. The whole town. And they still do. Except me. I'm lapsed, you might say. This happened back in the late '50s. I was just startin out as a builder, doin whatever I could get.

The church roof was real bad. It was leakin buckets. A boat, it woulda sunk. The priest asked in a sermon as a matter of fact if people could help—everyone was pretty poor in those days, at least nothin like now—so me and my two men, we volunteered. We did the job. Not a small job either. Not an easy job. Scaffolding. All that. Took us a week about.

After a little while—the Father didn't say anything—I submitted a bill. Just the materials, you know, no labor. He thanked me. And then nothin happened.

Coupla months went by, I asked him about it. "Oh," he says, "It's in the works. Don't worry."

Coupla more months went by. I didn't like to say anything. Finally I submitted another bill. Father always smiled when I'd catch his eye. Like he was blessin me.

Well, about a whole year went by. I submitted another bill. Third bill. I didn't like to be rude. But. You know.

Nothing happened. What're you gonna do? You know? Sooner or later. So one day I stayed till I was the last one comin out of Mass. I asked the Father.

"Oh," he says, "there's nothing I can do. We don't have any

money. I'll have to put in for it to the Bishop in Fall River. Don't worry. Everything's going to be all right."

I thought, Well, okay, that's progress. I waited a few months. Nothin happened. I submitted another bill, just to remindim. Still nothin happened.

So I waited around for Father after Mass. I says, "I hate to be a pain but I need that $1,200."

He looked like he couldn't remember who I was. Then he says, "Oh, there's nothin I can do. We don't have any money. I put in to Fall River, but the Bishop said they don't have any money either, and he's going to have to put in to the Cardinal up in Boston. I've done everything I can. There's nothing more we can do right now but just be patient and wait. Have a little faith, my son. Maybe we should just consider it a little contribution to the church."

I says, "Fuck you, Father. Fuck the Bishop in Fall River. And fuck the fucking Cardinal up in Boston too."

I started to walk out. Then I had this vision of my sister and my wife and my mother and my aunts and my grandmother and my great-grandmother. I could see them clear as day, I could hear them too. They were like a chorus, like a choir, and they were all screaming, "For God's sake, take that back. You'll be struck by lightning."

I got really scared. But I was even madder than I was scared. I didn't want to take it back. I figured I was dead anyway. I walked out the door, I went down the steps. When I got to the sidewalk I took a chance and looked up at the sky. Nothing there but sun. I says, "God, I just want my money. Just the materials. We did the work for free. For You."

Nothin happened so I kept on home. I didn't get struck by lightning, and I never set foot in that fucking church again. I never got paid either.

Ways Old and New

For some reason Memorial Day is the worst of all now. It used to be my favorite holiday, start of the season. It was a very tranquil weekend. We always looked forward to it. I always thought of it as the first day of summer. The flowers just coming out. All that new green. End of the bleak spring rains. The sun at last. Almost warm enough to swim. And some of the people you knew would be back. And you were glad to see them. But in general it was pensive—very laid back, as they say now.

People are more rude than they ever were. They're so loud and insulting, it's almost as if they come here to show how pushy they can be. It gets worse every year. And you can't tell what they're going to be like by looking at them. Once they're in your house you've got to put up with them. And they always leave a mess. You wouldn't believe some of the things I've had to clean up. The last few years have been pretty discouraging. I don't even like to go out on the street.

This year I just put up a NO VACANCY sign and worked in my garden the whole weekend. It was almost like old times. Of course in those days we always went to the cemetery. And laid flowers and tidied my parents' plot. And my husband's. I haven't done that in years. Maybe I'll go out next year. It's a nice walk. This year I actually enjoyed the whole weekend.

Then Tuesday everything was back to normal. Whatever that means.

No Escape for Yours Truly

Long time no see is right. I suppose you've been here all along, stuck in your rut. Me, I've been in Labrador because there's no one there—empty forest, bears and wolves. I figured I'd be better off. You know what a hermit I am. I'd go days, whole weeks, without seeing a soul. I says to myself, This is real life.

You'll laugh when you hear how I happened to move back to P-town. I don't understand it myself. That's a fact. I'm still trying to figure it out.

I never stop for hitchhikers. Never! I dislike men anyway, I'm afraid of them. You know me. I'm a realist.

Well. So. One night it was raining—not hard but I could see the silver drops coming down—there was a girl waiting at the start of Three Mile Bridge. It's really only a causeway that strings the hummocks together. Swampy ponds all around, dead stumps sticking up and low cement walls like some sort of mole-run about exactly two cars wide. She was just standing there. She didn't even hold out her thumb.

Maybe that's why I stopped. I says to myself, This person's just like me, she's shy, she's obstinate, she even looks like me twenty years ago—sweatshirt, old jeans, work shoes, black bangs cut very short. We're just two women out in the rain at night. The only difference is I've got a car.

She got in. Didn't say one word. Too proud even to say thanks was my first impression. So I says, "Are you going to Warton?"

This was just a stupid friendly question. Warton's all there was ahead, one store and a gas pump. It's a dead end. To get anywhere else you have to go back. One road in, same road out. And the locals never leave. They don't know there's anywhere else. The women are ancient. The men have beards. I never learned a single name.

She didn't say anything. Her posture sort of said, Don't tamper with me. I may be in your car, but I'm no business of yours, and I'm not beholden neither.

"Are you wet?" I says. I turned the heater on and drove a while. You have to pay attention. It's oppressive even in daylight. At night it's claustrophobic, like a tunnel.

I was annoyed when she wouldn't speak. Every time I glanced at her I would catch her glancing away. Of course she knew I was a stranger. And I knew she knew it. And she knew I knew she knew it. People are very standoffish up there. That was what I liked about the place, but all of a sudden I began to get nervous. She had a face like a cloud, different every time I looked.

Finally I began to sense she really despised me. You know these intimations you get, intuitions I mean. It didn't seem fair. She didn't know who I was, she probably never heard the word gay in her life, but automatically she had a terrible opinion of me. She was just full of disdain. Good old country contempt. I could feel it. I began to wilt, the way I always do. The worst of it was, I half agreed with her. Then I decided for once I wasn't going to give in to it. I was going to stand up for myself. I wasn't going to lie either.

I'm not a native," I says, "but I still like it here. It's a nice quiet dull place suitable to myself."

She kept in her corner, gave me not a sign. She had the steadiest eyes I've ever seen, like once she'd sized me up nothing I could ever do would change her mind. You know the type. Like they don't live in the same world you do.

Why I was so determined to win her over I do not know, but I began making small talk, chitchat about my life and hard times, with some discretion, a few omissions—at least at first. But once I got going I couldn't stop. I didn't even want to stop. All my cats got out of the bag and ran every which-way. The more I said the more I had to explain, even to myself. I began to wonder what I'd say next, I wasn't even worried.

She kept absolutely aloof, as if she had no use for the whole human race, unless you happened to come from Warton. I went right on trying to justify myself. I told her all my childhood disillusions, all my youthful miseries, my humiliations and disasters with men, my crushes on women. It all sounded like a great big nothing. I was almost groveling, and it had no effect on her whatever. None. That got my goat. I guess I felt insulted. And what did I want a friend for anyway? I don't even drink coffee anymore.

I began to rant. I told her my most detested secrets, I babbled baby talk and made-up rhymes. I thought, I'll get a rise out of this snot. I sang her a dirty ditty I didn't even know I knew, I was conducting with both hands like it was some kind of polka.

Imagine the irony when I caught on she was just torturing me before the end. I was stunned, I was mortified to think I had moved a thousand miles up here to be married by a psychopath. Ha, ha. You know I mean murdered. And by the first and only hitchhiker I ever picked up in my whole life. And a woman at that!

I blithered and blathered faster and faster, the way it turns into double-talk and you start to wonder what you're saying and then you wonder who's saying it? I was three sheets to the wind, not a drop had I had. I was convinced if I could fill this void between us it would stave off some disaster worse than all my worst imaginings.

Half the time she was terrified, clutching the seat, staring straight ahead. I'd got to weaving and it was hot, hot. The heater was going full blast, the windows were shut. I was drenched with sweat. I'd've given anything to be able to stop and rest.

Finally of course I realized what a fool I was, how as usual it was all my own fault, that she would gladly be friendly if I gave her half a chance. Behind that stony face and those black eyes I began to sense her sympathy, some huge backwoods tact, but I still couldn't shut up. Strange to say, by that time, I felt like I was just too much of a sophisticate, this grey-haired lady from Baltimore up in the far sticks, and anyway it was too late. There was just too much I had to spill, things I hadn't even remembered yet. All I know is, I wasn't going to leave anything unsaid. After a certain point it was pure defiance on my part, and her patience only made me madder.

I grew very menacing, I could feel myself swelling up. The car was careening, I'd sneer at the road every once in a while. I got out my tobacco pouch and filled my pipe and got it lit, then I coughed a lapful of embers over us, we were beating ourselves.

It was black as pitch. We were like a little capsule falling down a well toward the middle of the earth. I never realized how small a car is. I forgot to turn the heater off, we were breathing up the same air. I could feel my hair bristling, our eyes locked and I actually snarled. She folded her arms and gave me an awful glare.

I thought, Someone's going to get killed here. But it only lasted a second, then we both looked away—in sheer exhaustion, to tell you the truth—and then I went back to driving again. I had no idea where we were. There are no landmarks out there. I thought, How long can this go on?

I had both hands on the wheel, like I always do, but I must have blinked, maybe I shut my eyes for a moment, just for relief from the tension, maybe I just tuned out, or fell asleep and dreamed, because next thing I knew a trailer truck—one of those endless ten-wheelers—was coming around a curve at us in the distance with its sidelights streaming behind like a comet. I was too paralyzed to put on the brakes. The headlights kept getting bigger and brighter, and bigger and brighter, then suddenly they merged in one huge blinding ball.

I swerved, she swerved us back, thank God. We went wrestling down the road about thirty miles an hour and never hit a thing.

I looked in the mirror. There was nothing there. There was nothing in front of us either. I'll never understand. You should have heard me trying to explain. I was a wreck, the car was creeping.

When the end of the bridge came in sight she couldn't wait to get the door open. She was all hunched over, ready to go. I thought she had to puke. The instant we hit dry land I stopped, she gave an awful moan and somersaulted down this little embankment. At the bottom she just jumped up and ran, it was still a mile to Warton.

I leaned across the seat and yelled after her, but she kept right on going, this Neanderthal hulk, straight into the thicket. I could hear this terrific cracking and snapping.

I heard that din in my dreams for a whole month before it dawned on me she was deaf. That was the day I decided to move back.

I don't say I'm not glad to be here.

Here I Am

I never thought I'd be sitting here again like this, drinking whiskey at the bar in the Bradford on a Sunday in the early afternoon, with the sun streaming through the windows and everybody else at the beach, the way Seth and I used to do.

I've hardly left the house in seven months, except for work and the A&P—but here I am. I didn't plan to do it. I just happened to be walking by, and came in.

It was the nice day that got me out. But the heart doesn't ache any less. It almost feels like Seth's sitting here beside me, but he's not. He was like my Siamese twin that got amputated. I never could tell who I was mourning for, myself or him. All those last days I lay in bed with him he shrank away. He was a big man but he ended up smaller than me. He said, "I'm going to leave you a bag of bones." We had to laugh, and then we had to cry. I learned what love was. We learned together.

I was happy with him every minute, our whole five years. My first two marriages were not exactly idyllic. Strange to realize that I was everything to a man, and him everything to me. Maybe that's why one of us had to die. I guess I'm glad it wasn't me. I don't think he could have stood it. I can stand it because I'm a woman, but I'm wizened inside. I can feel it. I don't look in the mirror anymore. I used to like to look good for him.

We both had a taste for the social life. Before we met we loved to be part of the action, go to parties, keep up with the gossip. He was a very warm person, very gregarious. When he laughed the rafters shook. People liked to be around him.

After we met though we hardly bothered with anybody but

each other. It was quite a switch, when you think of it, to be going down to the Bradford for a couple of hours once a week and not even notice who else was there, unless they came over to say hello. We only talked to each other anymore. We never got enough of each other's thoughts. I knew we were lucky, but I didn't know how lucky.

He was never married. He said he never had the heart for it, he always knew something would go wrong. He had a lot of miserable love affairs, he always messed up, and at some point before he even came to town he just said the hell with it. He'd been alone a long time when I met him, but he had no hesitation at all about commitment. Right away he asked me if I wanted to. I said I didn't care if we did or didn't, whatever he wanted was fine with me. It wouldn't have meant anything. We couldn't have got any more married than we already were.

Now there's Karen and her fancy new boyfriend. When she broke up with Burke he moped around for a whole winter playing the pinball machine, while she lived on the beach in Puerto Rico with this new guy, and nearly got blown away by a hurricane, and when they came back and began drinking in here Burke left town.

For years she matched him Stoli for Stoli, from the time they got off work at eight till closing every night of the week. They had synchronized shifts, and they never stayed away. You'd see them arm-in-arm lurching home at two in the morning. She said to me one night, "I don't understand men. Do you understand men? Someday I'm going to understand men."

Night in, night out, Burke talked, she listened. One mouth, two ears. He was a born pessimist, but alcohol made him morose. She was always trying to cheer him up. Janine said to her one time, "Let him be unhappy. If that's what he likes let him. You can't make him over."

Janine's had a million boyfriends—used to, I mean. She calls them all "Love," even when there's a horde of them around her.

No hard feelings with any of them. "Done's done," she says. She takes what comes.

Now Karen's all ears for this new mouth. Only it's afternoon instead of night and he's drinking beer instead of vodka, and so is she. She hates beer. Whatever she can do she does, but it looks like work to me. I wonder what she thinks it means, to understand men. She never gets depressed at least.

And there's Johnny Puto. I haven't seen him in a while either. Years actually. He's back for a week with his ex and their two sons, only the fifteen year old met up with some older girl and disappeared the minute they got here yesterday. Johnny hasn't changed a bit. He's still off in the stratosphere. He says, "They know where the tent is, they'll come back when they feel like it. So long as it doesn't rain snow they're OK."

The mother's frantic they're doing drugs, not to mention whatever else, and the thirteen year old looks sullen enough to run off himself if she'd just go to the ladies room for two seconds. He's tired of cokes.

I don't heed much anymore. Happiness is selfish. I never even knew what the word meant till I met Seth. I was completely happy for five years. At fifty-six, what can I expect? What can I even want? I might as well mourn for everybody.

All that sun out there. These few sad sacks in here. They don't even know how they are. This is their normal. Nobody knows anything until it's too late. For the first time in my life though I have no regrets. Seth said I made him a good man. It was easy. He had it in him for me. I never even had to try.

If you don't meet somebody, it probably wasn't meant to be. You can't bemoan fate. Anyway there's been too much death and destruction these last few years. All my AIDS friends died, one by one. It didn't half hurt until today. I cried at the time, Seth and I went to all the funerals, but it just made our love all the more private. The world was the way it was. But it wasn't us. When I walked in here an hour ago I realized how many were gone. All of them. Every one.

I guess I'll sit a while. I'll make a list. I'll write down their names like things to do. There's always more humanity when you're alone.

Where Does the Time Go

Good question. A lot of thinking people these days are concerned with time and where they'll be.

You reach my age, you wonder. Just yesterday I had a nightmare. First I couldn't sleep, then I dreamed it was spring. Green leaves, warm breezes. I felt like a boy again.

Then that faded out and I was on a tight-line, you know, over the air. My arms were out like a gull. I was looking down. Nothing there. I knew I couldn't fly.

I said to myself, How did I get here? Is all this just a dream?

A voice says, This is no dream.

I says, This here is a dream and I want to wake up.

He says, You just want to pretend this is not real because it's a dream.

Aw, shut up, I says. You're just a dream yourself.

But you're the dreamer, he says. You just want to pretend you're awake.

I says, You can't tell if I'm awake or not.

He says, Neither can you.

I thought to myself, If I say, Life goes on spinning whether we know it or not, he'll say, Yeah, but you can't even tell who's dreaming who, much less who's doing the spinning. You just want to pretend you think you've got a grip on it.

I thought to myself, I'm not having any arguments with myself that I can't win.

Just leave me alone, I says. I want to go to sleep.

Weak as it was it worked. I slept through like a baby.

Pat de Groot

This collation of forty-two voices speaks in the time of Provincetown's change from dying fishery, art colony and refuge of mavericks who loved freedom above money, to gentrified gay condo-ville, pectoral pomp and center of AIDS resistence, a demographic mix unique and rich—dominant Portuguese and once dominant Yankee natives, die-hard fishermen, jacks of all trades impoversihed by skyrocketing rents, remnants of the straight bar culture, barnacles from the year one, their old world seemingly suddenly submerged in the new tide of gay guest houses, chic shops, drag festivals, rehab and building booms, political and economic rule by women, cults of healing and self-acceptance, multifarious 12-steppers, unregenerate hedonists of every stripe, the omnipresent Grand Guignol of HIV, and, uniting its disparate citizens, a huge chauvinism of place, personality and indepentdent mores, an enduring love of the town, a.k.a. Utopia, Either Way, or The One and Only Place to Live.